YORK NOTES

Middlemarch

George Eliot

Note by Dr Julian Cowley

Longman   York Press

Dr Julian Cowley is hereby identified as author of this work in accordance with Section 77 of the Copyright, Designs and Patents Act 1988

YORK PRESS
322 Old Brompton Road, London SW5 9JH

PEARSON EDUCATION LIMITED
Edinburgh Gate, Harlow,
Essex CM20 2JE, United Kingdom
Associated companies, branches and representatives throughout the world

First published 2000
Third impression 2002

ISBN 0-582-42450-X

Designed by Vicki Pacey
Phototypeset by Gem Graphics, Trenance, Mawgan Porth, Cornwall
Colour reproduction and film output by Spectrum Colour
Produced by Pearson Education North Asia Limited, Hong Kong

CONTENTS

PART ONE

INTRODUCTION

HOW TO STUDY A NOVEL

Studying a novel on your own requires self-discipline and a carefully thought-out work plan in order to be effective.

- You will need to read the novel more than once. Start by reading it quickly for pleasure, then read it slowly and thoroughly.

- On your second reading make detailed notes on the plot, characters and themes of the novel. Further readings will generate new ideas and help you to memorise the details of the story.

- Some of the characters will develop as the plot unfolds. How do your responses towards them change during the course of the novel?

- Think about how the novel is narrated. From whose point of view are events described?

- A novel may or may not present events chronologically: the time-scheme may be a key to its structure and organisation.

- What part do the settings play in the novel?

- Are words, images or incidents repeated so as to give the work a pattern? Do such patterns help you to understand the novel's themes?

- Identify what styles of language are used in the novel.

- What is the effect of the novel's ending? Is the action completed and closed, or left incomplete and open?

- Does the novel present a moral and just world?

- Cite exact sources for all quotations, whether from the text itself or from critical commentaries. Wherever possible find your own examples from the novel to back up your opinions.

- Always express your ideas in your own words.

This York Note offers an introduction to *Middlemarch* and cannot substitute for close reading of the text and the study of secondary sources.

The writer Virginia Woolf (1882–1941) called *Middlemarch* 'one of the few English novels written for grown-up people'. Many other readers have agreed that George Eliot's greatest novel ranks with the highest achievements in all literature. It is subtitled 'A Study of Provincial Life', but that simple description is deceptive. Within its pages there is vivid depiction of English life in the early 1830s, but the scope of *Middlemarch* is far wider. It is a study of selfishness and self-sacrifice, a story of human aspiration and frustration, of hope and compromise.

George Eliot made a major contribution to our sense that novels are not only a form of entertainment, but can also be works of art. *Middlemarch* is challenging and fulfilling in equal measure. It is a large novel, but is always skilfully controlled. It was composed with great care, and its elaborately patterned structure enriches the experience of reading. It offers a panoramic view of a society in transition, touching on those large historical forces which produce social change. Embedded in this broad picture are intimate love stories, developed with evident sympathy and portrayed with psychological subtlety.

Middlemarch is also a novel about the quest for knowledge and the limits of human understanding. It is about the various forms of power that individuals exercise over one another. It looks at how the past shapes the present, and investigates the capacity of an individual to contribute to the improvement of the world as a place in which to live.

These are grand concerns, outlined here in abstract terms. But entering the world of *Middlemarch* you encounter the beautiful and passionately idealistic Dorothea Brooke, the intense young doctor Tertius Lydgate, and the dashing dilettante Will Ladislaw. You follow the entanglement of their lives with the scholarly Edward Casaubon, the graceful yet shallow Rosamond Vincy, and the hypocritical banker Nicholas Bulstrode. Many other characters are met along the way. They lodge in the mind to make *Middlemarch* a truly memorable work of literary art.

PART TWO

Summaries & Commentaries

Middlemarch was originally planned as two separate stories, one concerning Lydgate, the other entitled 'Miss Brooke'. The first 18 chapters fuse these two strands. *Middlemarch* appeared initially between December 1871 and December 1872 in eight half-volume instalments, issued at two-monthly intervals with the final three instalments appearing monthly. It was subsequently compiled into four volumes. Novels throughout the nineteenth century were usually issued in three-volume editions. A cheaper edition, the 'Guinea Edition' was published in March 1873.

This Note uses the Penguin Classics *Middlemarch*, 1994, edited by Rosemary Ashton. It is based on the second edition, which appeared in May 1874, the last one thoroughly corrected by George Eliot.

In 1994, an adaptation of the novel for BBC Television generated such interest that Middlemarch reached the top of the paperback bestseller list.

All the textual variants arising from the author's revisions can be found in the Clarendon Edition, edited by David Carroll (1986). *George Eliot's Middlemarch Notebooks* (University of California Press) is a transcription by John Clark Pratt and Victor E. Neufeldt of the notebooks which trace George Eliot's composition of the novel.

Synopsis

It is 1829. Dorothea and Celia Brooke are sisters who live with their uncle Arthur Brooke at Tipton Grange, near the town of Middlemarch. Sir James Chettam, a baronet who owns a neighbouring estate, wishes to marry Dorothea. Dorothea, however, is an immensely serious young woman, and she chooses instead to marry the scholarly rector of Lowick, Edward Casaubon, who is about thirty years her senior.

On a preliminary visit to her new home, Lowick Manor, Dorothea meets Casaubon's young cousin, Will Ladislaw. The acquaintance is renewed in Rome, where Mr and Mrs Casaubon are spending their honeymoon. Casaubon shows more interest in pursuit of his studies than in his new wife, and although she remains loyal to her husband Dorothea is drawn to Ladislaw. The young man has relied upon financial support from his cousin. Appalled at the incongruity of the marriage, Ladislaw determines that on his return to England he will seek to live independently. He unsettles Dorothea by casting doubt on the value of her husband's work.

Meanwhile, a young doctor called Tertius Lydgate has joined the Middlemarch community. He is struck by the beauty of Rosamond Vincy, daughter of the town's mayor. Her brother, Fred Vincy, is troubled by debt, but he anticipates an inheritance from his elderly uncle, Peter Featherstone. Fred hopes to marry Mary Garth, who is looking after the old man.

Nicholas Bulstrode, a banker, allocates Lydgate supervision of the new hospital. The doctor pleases Bulstrode by securing the hospital chaplaincy for Walter Tyke, the banker's favoured candidate. In doing so, Lydgate frustrates the aspirations of his own friend, Mr Farebrother.

Fred's inability to settle his debt places the financial burden upon Caleb Garth, Mary's father, who has acted as security for the amount owed. Trying unsuccessfully to resolve his dilemma, Fred falls ill. During the time that Lydgate is treating Fred's illness, his relationship with Rosamond develops.

On their return home, Dorothea and Casaubon learn that Celia has become engaged to Chettam. Soon afterwards, Casaubon suffers a heart attack, and as a consequence his activities are circumscribed. Lydgate becomes engaged to Rosamond Vincy.

As Featherstone is dying he asks Mary Garth to destroy the most recent will he has made. She refuses. After his death, his relatives are dismayed to learn that his estate has been left to a stranger, Joshua Rigg, the old man's secret son.

Casaubon is alarmed at the growing friendship between his wife and Ladislaw. Mr Brooke, who has political ambitions as a reformer, becomes proprietor of a newspaper and asks Ladislaw to edit it. Casaubon tells his cousin that if he takes the post he will no longer be welcome at Lowick Manor. Ladislaw is defiant.

Caleb Garth's straitened financial situation is alleviated when he is invited to manage estates for both Chettam and Brooke. Fred Vincy passes his degree, but Garth suggests he might assist him rather than becoming a clergyman.

Casaubon asks Dorothea to continue his work in the event of his death. She initially refuses to make that commitment. On reflection she feels she must, but before she can discuss the matter further she finds her husband dead. A codicil added to his will stipulates that if Dorothea marries Ladislaw she will forfeit the Lowick estate. Immersing herself in practical matters, Dorothea offers support for the hospital, and on Lydgate's recommendation, appoints Farebrother as rector of Lowick.

Brooke retires from politics after an inept attempt to campaign. He dismisses Ladislaw. Ladislaw has no knowledge of Casaubon's stipulation, but he feels it would be improper for him to be seen as a potential suitor for his late cousin's wife, and he keeps his distance.

Bulstrode purchases Stone Court, formerly Featherstone's home, from Joshua Rigg. Rigg's stepfather, John Raffles, arrives and starts to extort money from the banker. It is revealed that Bulstrode's money derived from marriage to Mrs Dunkirk, a wealthy older woman, who owned a pawnbroking business, apparently receiving stolen goods. Prior to the marriage, Bulstrode concealed the fact that Mrs Dunkirk's runaway daughter had been traced. This concealment meant that the substantial inheritance would be his.

Lydgate has incurred heavy debts, and his marriage grows increasingly strained. Rosamond suffers a miscarriage. Ladislaw visits the Lydgates, and learns of the codicil in his cousin's will. Raffles encounters Ladislaw and reveals that Mrs Dunkirk's daughter was the young man's mother and that Bulstrode has deprived him of his rightful inheritance. Ladislaw is appalled to discover that his family history has involved dishonourable business activities. Bulstrode offers an annual allowance to Ladislaw, who rejects the offer as an insult.

Lydgate seeks financial assistance from the troubled banker. Bulstrode refuses to help him, and reveals that he is withdrawing support from the hospital. The same day, Garth visits Bulstrode to tell him that he has found Raffles by the roadside, clearly very ill, and has taken him to Stone Court. An arrangement had been made that Fred Vincy should manage that property, under Garth's supervision. Raffles has told Garth of the banker's past, and as a matter of honour he now severs the business connection between them. Later, Mrs Bulstrode persuades Garth to restore the arrangement, which enables Fred to marry Mary, and to become a successful farmer.

Bulstrode summons Lydgate to attend to Raffles. In order to win the doctor's allegiance, he writes a cheque to clear his considerable debts. Lydgate gives specific instructions for the care of Raffles, whom he believes should survive this bout of illness. Bulstrode fails to convey these instructions to his housekeeper, and as a consequence of the opium and brandy she administers the man dies.

Lydgate feels uneasy. Bulstrode is relieved that the extortion has come to an end. But Raffles had disclosed the banker's hidden past to Bambridge, the horse-dealer, and it soon becomes the focus for Middlemarch gossip. Bulstrode's reputation is destroyed, and Lydgate is implicated in the allegations.

Dorothea has faith in Lydgate and seeks to clear his name. She writes a cheque, allowing him to clear his debt to Bulstrode. Lydgate and Rosamond move to London, where he becomes a successful practitioner, and they have children. After his death, at fifty, Rosamond marries a wealthy older doctor.

Ladislaw returns to Middlemarch. He and Dorothea acknowledge their love for one another. She gives up Lowick Manor and they marry, to the dismay of her friends and relatives. The couple move to London, and have children. Ladislaw becomes a reforming politician. In time, they are welcomed back to Middlemarch, and Dorothea's son eventually inherits Tipton Grange.

PRELUDE

The novel begins with reference to Saint Theresa of Avila, whose 'passionate, ideal nature demanded an epic life' (p. 3). Many women have aspired to transcend the limitations imposed upon their lives, but few have achieved that goal.

The novel is subtitled 'A Study of Provincial Life', but the 'Prelude' takes us far from provincial England, to sixteenth-century Spain and the ecstatic visions of Saint Theresa. Theresa stands as a **type** for women who have aspired to transcend the limits of their circumstances, and to make a positive contribution to the world. Dorothea Brooke is just such a woman. Eliot uses the word **epic** to denote a life conducted in heroic style, engaged with grand issues.

Throughout *Middlemarch*, Eliot directs our attention to both the particular and the general, to specific cases and to types of character or behaviour. That process is established here. We are now prepared to understand Dorothea in the light of Saint Theresa. Saint Theresa benefited from the 'coherent social faith and order' (p. 3) of an ardently Christian society. Eliot's contemporaries were haunted by the sense that such simple faith was no longer tenable. She shared a view, widespread amongst intellectuals, that Christianity no longer provided an overarching framework for understanding life (see Historical Background: Loss of Faith).

Middlemarch is a novel which contains social criticism. The 'Prelude' alludes to a repressive uniformity in women's fashions and tastes which stifles development of individual personality.

Saint Theresa Saint Teresa of Avila (1515–82), Spanish visionary, who established a religious order

epos epic poem

BOOK ONE: 'MISS BROOKE'

CHAPTER 1   **The Brooke sisters and their uncle Arthur are introduced**

Dorothea and Celia Brooke, teenage sisters, have lived for a year with their uncle, Arthur Brooke, at Tipton Grange, near the town of

Middlemarch. Their parents died when they were 'about twelve years old' (p. 8). They subsequently lived with an English and then a Swiss family. Dorothea is physically attractive and clever, but Celia is generally recognised to have more common sense. Dorothea is a pious Christian. Her moral seriousness is evident from her concern to improve living conditions for local labourers. She is fascinated by greatness, and especially by intellectual achievement. Her intensity is seen as a potential obstacle to marriage, and Mr Brooke is blamed by acquaintances for not introducing into his household 'some middle-aged lady as a guide and companion to his nieces' (p. 10).

At Celia's request, the sisters look at jewellery left to them by their mother. Dorothea says her sister can have it all, but then decides to keep an emerald ring and matching bracelet.

> Each chapter begins with a quotation. Here George Eliot quotes from a sixteenth-century play. Sometimes these **epigrams** are invented. In all cases, they indicate a major thematic concern of the chapter. Here the concern is evidently with restriction of opportunities for women to perform benevolent acts of real social importance.

> *Middlemarch* was set forty years in the past at the time of composition. This allowed George Eliot to make even her first readers aware of processes of social change. In this chapter we are presented with a society that is clearly stratified in terms of social class. A major concern of the novel is the advancement of the middle class, the class of business and the professions, which was growing increasingly wealthy, and was securing more and more social power. The novel's title may perhaps be taken as a **punning** allusion to the march of the middle.

> Eliot uses contrast to develop characterisation. Dorothea and Celia are delineated in part through their differences. Celia appears lightweight beside her earnest sister, but she is more popular and is considered to have more common sense.

> Clothing is a conventional means of signalling gender roles. Dorothea's lack of interest in fashion indicates that she is not content with conventional femininity. She has no wish to be merely

an ornament, a pretty addition to a man's possessions. Accordingly, she dresses as simply as possible.

Dorothea is fascinated by greatness of the kind which changes the course of history or leaves an indelible mark on the world. George Eliot's novel is critical of the customary belief that such greatness is the province of men, and can be achieved by women only if they are prepared, like Saint Theresa, to become martyrs.

Pascal's *Pensées* defence of Christian beliefs by French philosopher Blaise Pascal (1623–1662), published posthumously in 1670
Jeremy Taylor (1613–1670), preacher and advocate of religious toleration
Mr Peel's late conduct on the Catholic Question Robert Peel (1788–1850), Home Secretary, who initially opposed Catholic Emancipation, then supported it
Hooker Richard Hooker (1554–1600), Anglican theologian
John Milton (1608–1674), poet, best known for the epic, *Paradise Lost*
Henrietta Maria (1605–69), wife of Charles I

CHAPTER 2   **A dinner party. Sir James Chettam shows interest in Dorothea, but she is fascinated by the scholarly Mr Casaubon**

At a dinner party hosted by Brooke, Sir James Chettam seeks to court Dorothea, but she is fascinated by the older Mr Casaubon. Casaubon wants someone to read to him in the evenings, as his scholarly work is causing his eyesight to fade. Dorothea is keen to assist. Chettam remarks to Celia that her sister is given to 'self-mortification'. Celia agrees that Dorothea 'likes giving up' (p. 18). Brooke argues that 'young ladies are too flighty' to be entrusted with weighty documents (p. 20).

After dinner, Celia remarks upon Casaubon's ugliness. Dorothea vehemently asserts that he is a distinguished man. Celia knows that Chettam is enamoured of her sister, but suspects that Dorothea's intellectual aspirations would make her an unsuitable match for the baronet.

The **epigram** from Miguel de Cervantes (1547–1616), which is concerned with distorted perception, prepares us for Dorothea's idealised view of Casaubon. It suggests that, like Don Quixote, she is deluding herself, while Celia is contrastingly direct and down-to-earth.

Brooke likes to display his learning, but it inevitably sounds rambling and confused. George Eliot contrasts his misguided displays of erudition with the taciturn presence of Casaubon, who is reputedly a formidable scholar. The characterisation of both is advanced by this contrast.

Similarly, characterisation of Dorothea is developed by placing her between two diametrically opposed suitors: Casaubon with his taste for cloistered seclusion, and Chettam with his energetic enjoyment of outdoor pursuits.

Although Brooke initially appears an amiable buffoon, his avuncular kindliness is cut through with assumptions of the inferior capabilities of women. As the consequences of such assumptions become increasingly serious for Dorothea, Brooke's foolishness appears less harmless.

Sir Humphry Davy (1778–1829), eminent scientist

Locke John Locke (1632–1704), philosopher

Adam Smith (1723–90), influential economist and champion of free trade

Southey Robert Southey (1774–1843), poet and historian

the Waldenses French religious sect persecuted as heretics

Wilberforce William Wilberforce (1759–1833), politician and philanthropist who campaigned against slavery

cochon de lait (French) suckling pig

pilulous resembling a small pill

Mawworm sanctimonious hypocrite, protagonist of Isaac Bickerstaffe's play *The Hypocrite* (1769)

CHAPTER 3   **Dorothea talks at length with Casaubon, and envisages marriage to him. Chettam presents her with a lapdog, which she rejects, but he pleases her with his proposal to build cottages for local labourers**

On the following day, Casaubon discusses with Dorothea his work on comparative mythology. He speaks of his need for companionship. Then he returns to his home at Lowick, five miles away.

Dorothea walks in the woods with Monk, her Great St Bernard dog, and contemplates marriage to Casaubon, suspecting a proposal is imminent. She encounters Chettam, who is riding. He offers her a puppy, which she haughtily rejects, suggesting it might be an appropriate gift for Celia.

He offers to realise Dorothea's pet project by building cottages for poor labourers on his estate. Regarding him as potential brother-in-law, she welcomes his beneficence and shows him plans she has prepared.

Further conversations with Casaubon deepen Dorothea's admiration. She reveres his seriousness, although she is disappointed by his lack of interest in her building projects. Chettam visits more often, and while Dorothea receives him with greater warmth, she is preoccupied with improving her mind in preparation for Casaubon's company.

Middlemarch is a work of literary **realism**, but it nonetheless relies upon the author's contrivance. Realism is the product of controlled artifice, even though it may seem to offer a transparent window through which to watch the world. An example of George Eliot's craft is evident in the contrast between the lapdog which Dorothea rejects, and the Great St Bernard she willingly takes for a walk. The Maltese puppy may be seen to correspond to the view that women are mere embellishments, superficially adorning a world run by men. The Great St Bernard, on the other hand, is well known as a working dog, effective in rescue operations. Its presence reflects Dorothea's desire to be useful, even to save others through her actions.

The narrator refers to Dorothea's 'soul-hunger' (p. 29), which motivates her to eschew the trivial and aspire to great deeds. She believes that marriage to Casaubon will elevate her, and she sees him as St Augustine. Later in the novel he is **ironically** cast by the painter Naumann as another important saint, Thomas Aquinas. By that point it has become very clear that Casaubon does not merit such comparisons. But remember that we have been invited to see Dorothea in the light of St Theresa. Is it possible for her life to justify that comparison?

> **Bossuet** Jacques Bénigne Bossuet (1627–1704), French bishop who
> advocated reconciliation of the Catholic and Protestant churches
> **Augustine** St Augustine (354–430), important figure in the history of
> Christianity
> **Rhamnus** coastal town near Athens with ancient ruins
> *custos rutulorum* (Latin) keeper of the public records
> *vide supra* (Latin) see above
> **Chloe ... Strephon** conventional names for young lovers in pastoral poetry
> *Female Scripture Characters* book by Frances Elizabeth King, published in
> 1813
> **Loudon's book** John Claudius Loudon (1783–1843) was a respected writer
> on gardens and farming
> **Oberlin** Johann Friedrich Oberlin (1740–1826), French Protestant reformer

CHAPTER 4   **The sisters discuss Chettam's marital intentions.
Brooke tells Dorothea that Casaubon hopes to marry
her. She replies that she would accept such a proposal**

Chettam has started the building project at Freshitt. The sisters have
visited the site. On the way home, they discuss the Baronet's character.
Celia insists that Sir James intends to marry Dorothea, not to become her
brother-in-law. Dorothea cries in response to this revelation, and grows
angry at the suggestion that she has shown fondness for him.

On their return home, Brooke announces that he has been to
Lowick Manor. Dorothea is excited by pamphlets, sent by Casaubon,
concerning the history of the early Church. Alone with Dorothea in the
library, Brooke reveals Casaubon's intention to propose marriage.
Dorothea declares she will accept such an offer. Her uncle mentions
that Chettam would make a good match, but she states emphatically her
preference for a husband who is 'above me in judgment and in all
knowledge' (p. 40). He then hands her a letter from Casaubon.

> The **epigram** which heads this chapter is unattributed because
> George Eliot has invented it. It serves the same function as an
> actual quotation, focusing our attention on a major thematic
> concern.

> Dorothea cries for the first time here. She sheds many more tears
> in the course of the novel. This is a measure of her intense,

passionate nature, but it also conforms to a stereotype of sensitive female vulnerability. Even the eminently practical Mary Garth, introduced in later chapters, is prone to weep. George Eliot is possibly presenting sensitivity as a positive aspect of female character. On the other hand, sobbing may be seen as a token of frustration, the response of someone with no power to control events.

The hanging of a sheep-stealer is a detail which reflects George Eliot's concern for historical accuracy in *Middlemarch*. Sheep-stealing ceased to be a capital offence in 1832.

nullifidian   a sceptic in religion
Romilly   Sir Samuel Romilly (1757–1818), legal reformer. He committed suicide
if Peel stays in   Peel resigned when Wellington's government fell in November 1830

CHAPTER 5   **Dorothea responds to Casaubon's letter. The next day she tells Celia of her intention to marry him. Celia is alarmed. Casaubon and Dorothea discuss their future**

After dinner, Dorothea retires to her room to write a reply to Casaubon, while Celia plays the piano. Brooke is discomforted by the promptness of her response. He fears that Chettam will be hurt, and knows that he will be blamed locally for the perversity of his niece's decision.

The next day, a letter from Casaubon announces he will attend for dinner. Celia provokes Dorothea with her criticisms of Casaubon, and is horrified to learn that her sister intends to marry him.

That evening, Dorothea talks at length with her prospective husband, pledging her dedication to his great work. It is decided that the wedding should take place within six weeks.

The narrator presents Casaubon's letter for us to read. Its flat, dry style effectively conveys the man. It was of course written, like the rest of the novel, by George Eliot, but incorporation of such documentary evidence is a standard device in literary **realism**. It appears to authenticate the events recounted by the narrator.

The quotation from Robert Burton (1577–1640) helps prepare for disclosure of the extent of Casaubon's poor health, which is soon to assume major significance for Dorothea. It is clear that the scholar regards marriage as an arrangement in which a wife subordinates her own interests to the needs of her husband. He affirms: 'The great charm of your sex is its capability of an ardent self-sacrificing affection, and herein we see its fitness to round and complete the existence of our own' (p. 50).

sonnets to Delia poems by Samuel Daniel (1562–1619)

CHAPTER 6   **Mrs Cadwallader arrives at Tipton Grange. She is outraged to hear of the engagement, and conveys the news to Chettam, who is still more appalled**

As Casaubon leaves Tipton Grange, Mrs Cadwallader, the rector's wife, arrives. She converses briefly with Mrs Fitchett, the lodge-keeper. Then, talking with Brooke, she comments upon Casaubon's presence. It is left to Celia, who arrives at the crucial moment, to reveal that Casaubon is Dorothea's fiancé. Mrs Cadwallader is outraged. She visits Chettam in order to break the shocking news. He receives it with 'concentrated disgust' (p. 58). Nonetheless, he resolves to go to Tipton Grange, to congratulate Dorothea, and to display his interest in her sister.

The word 'disgust' (p. 48) was used in the previous chapter to convey Celia's feelings at the prospect of the marriage. It is an emotive word, but one which recurs here to convey the adverse response to this ill-judged match. The strength of the reaction amongst her friends and relatives indicates the degree to which Dorothea is idealising Casaubon. It is already difficult to avoid concluding that she is mistaken.

Mrs Cadwallader is a witty character, who introduces an element of humour into the novel. She comes from an upper-class family but has married a poor clergyman. The marriage has been successful, but Mrs Cadwallader's faith in her class, and disparagement of those engaged in business and commerce, seem a little out of date in this world where money is increasingly linked to power.

uncommuted tithe produce equivalent to one-tenth of income paid as tax

Thirty-nine Articles the essential doctrine of the Church of England

a Saturday Pie a dish concocted from left-overs

the Sessions criminal court

varium et mutabile semper (Latin) fickle and ever-changing

Stoddart probably Sir John Stoddart (1773–1856), conservative newspaper proprietor

the Moravian Brethren religious sect formed in Saxony in 1722

the Seven Sages ancient Greek philosophers

Lord Tapir ... Lord Megatherium the tapir is a mammal related to the rhinoceros; the megatherium is an extinct creature, resembling a sloth

Sappho's apple Sappho (625–565BC), Greek poet. In one of her poems she compares a young virgin to an unplucked apple

CHAPTER 7   **Casaubon spends more time with Dorothea, who expresses her desire to assist with his scholarly work**

In preparation for the forthcoming marriage, Casaubon spends considerable time at Tipton Grange, although he secretly looks forward to returning to his work, the 'Key to all Mythologies' (p. 63). Dorothea emphasises her desire to assist him.

Dorothea is keen to learn Latin and Greek: 'Those provinces of masculine knowledge seemed to her a standing-ground from which all truth could be seen more truly' (p. 64). Her blinkered view of Casaubon arises from her ignorance, and that ignorance is evidently a consequence of the limited education allowed to her as a woman. Mr Brooke, her guardian, repeats his often stated view that 'deep studies', such as classics or mathematics, are 'too taxing for a woman'. He espouses the patriarchal prejudice that 'there is a lightness about the feminine mind' (p. 65).

The narrator reflects patriarchal prejudice in the comment that 'she wished, poor child, to be wise herself' (p. 64), but this is an **ironic** voice. George Eliot is implicitly criticising assumptions which relegate women to a child-like dependency upon male accomplishments.

The chapter ends with the narrator's observation that 'it is a narrow mind which cannot look at a subject from various points of view' (p. 66). *Middlemarch* is both technically and thematically engaged with the need to understand people and events from 'various points of view', offering different interpretations. There is no single key to understanding, yet that is what Casaubon hopes to discover. His labours are based upon a fundamental misapprehension, an outmoded conception of the nature of the world. They will bear no fruit, and in the course of the novel they will be consigned to the past.

Piacer e popone... (Italian) Pleasure and melons want the same weather

Gluck Christophe Gluck (1714–87), composer

Mozart Wolfgang Amadeus Mozart (1756–91), composer

Henry of Navarre in 1593 he converted to Catholicism and became Henry IV of France

CHAPTER 8   **Chettam's adverse response to the engagement is intensified when he witnesses the couple together at Tipton Grange**

Chettam visits Tipton and witnesses Dorothea with Casaubon. He is astonished at their engagement. He holds Brooke culpable for failing to steer his niece away from the match, and visits the Cadwalladers in the hope that some intervention might be made. He expresses to the rector his distaste for Casaubon. The rector extols the scholar's positive qualities and points out that his wife's family opposed her marriage to him, but Chettam remains unhappy. Still, he continues the building project, and finds that his conversations with Dorothea are more relaxed and pleasurable than when he hoped to marry her.

Cadwallader remarks that Casaubon is 'very good to his poor relations' (p. 69). This point later assumes greater significance with the introduction of Will Ladislaw. Ladislaw is caught up in a submerged web of family relationships. Casaubon's aunt Julia became Ladislaw's grandmother.

As Cadwallader puts it: 'His mother's sister made a bad match – a Pole, I think – lost herself – at any rate was disowned by her family'

(p. 69). There are numerous examples in the novel of marriages which might fall into the category of 'a bad match'.

Xisuthrus the equivalent to Noah in Babylonian mythology
Fee-fo-fum an ogre in fairy-tales

chapter 9   **The Brookes visit Casaubon's home, where Dorothea chooses her boudoir. They meet Will Ladislaw**

Mr Brooke and his nieces visit Lowick Manor, which is to be Dorothea's home. Celia finds the house's melancholy air dispiriting, but Dorothea is elated at the building's chaste and studious atmosphere. Following Celia's prompting, Dorothea takes for her boudoir the room that once belonged to Casaubon's mother.

Dorothea is introduced to Mr Tucker, the curate, who assures her that the local cottages are well maintained. They meet a young man with a sketchbook, whom Celia had earlier noticed in the garden. He is introduced as Will Ladislaw, grandson of Casaubon's aunt Julia. He displays 'a pouting air of discontent' (p. 79). Casaubon confides to Brooke that he is concerned about his young cousin's lack of direction in life, his aimless pursuit of 'culture' (p. 81).

Dorothea and Celia respond differently to Lowick Manor, and to the portrait of Casaubon's aunt. This reflects their different characters, but it also illustrates the important role played in *Middlemarch* by multiple points of view, and divergent interpretations.

The narrator wryly observes that 'a woman dictates before marriage in order that she may have an appetite for submission afterwards' (p. 73). But Dorothea's inclination to self-sacrifice makes her submissive even before marriage. She succumbs to Celia's persuasion in selecting her boudoir, and in doing so she commits herself to occupy a decidedly feminine space. The library, on the other hand, is emphatically her husband's domain.

Renaissance-Correggiosities reference to the work of Antonio da Correggio (1494–1534), painter
the good French King Henry IV of France

Aeolian harp musical instrument activated by the wind
a Bruce or a Mungo Park James Bruce (1730–94), and Mungo Park
(1771–1806), explorers of Africa
Chatterton Thomas Chatterton (1752–70), poet
Churchill Charles Churchill (1731–64), poet

CHAPTER 10 **Brooke hosts a dinner party, where Rosamond Vincy
and Mr Lydgate are discussed. Dorothea meets
Lydgate. Soon afterwards she marries Casaubon and
they travel to Rome**

Six days later, Casaubon mentions that his cousin, Will Ladislaw, has
departed for the Continent. The narrator argues against passing hasty
judgement on Casaubon, and suggests that we should try to perceive
things from his point of view. The honeymoon will take the couple to
Rome, the principal motive evidently being Casaubon's desire to visit the
Vatican library.

Brooke hosts a dinner party for local dignitaries, including the
mayor. The men discuss women, and Mr Chichely expresses his
preference for Miss Vincy, the mayor's daughter, who conforms to his
taste for a 'blond, with a certain gait, and a swan neck' (p. 89). Mrs
Cadwallader, Lady Chettam, and the widow of Colonel Renfrew discuss
medical matters, including the health of the prospective bridegroom.
They also talk of the new doctor, Mr Lydgate, who is said to be a
gentleman, and 'wonderfully clever' (p. 91). Lydgate and Dorothea
converse.

Soon afterwards, Dorothea marries Casaubon, and they travel to
Rome.

> Point of view is an issue once again. The narrator argues against
> passing judgement on Casaubon too hastily, and suggests that we
> should try to perceive things from his angle. Is this a serious
> request? We have recently learnt of the 'disgust' generated by news
> of the engagement, and the passionate Ladislaw presents an
> energetic contrast to his cousin. The narrator is surely issuing a
> considerable challenge in asking us to extend sympathy to the
> scholar. We may detect irony; or we may feel that this narrator is
> not always to be trusted or taken at face value.

The concern with variant interpretations, arising from different points of view, is pursued in the rest of the chapter, with the discussion of female attractiveness, and of Lydgate. Rosamond, who exhibits signs of femininity which meet with patriarchal approval, later becomes a decorative wife for Lydgate. The doctor, on the other hand, is deemed 'wonderfully clever', as is Dorothea. Their meeting, soon before her fateful marriage, raises the possibility of an alternative marital course both might have taken. Would Lydgate and Dorothea have been a 'bad match'? Near the start of the chapter, the narrator seems to caution against such speculation: 'Among all forms of mistake, prophecy is the most gratuitous' (p. 84).

The dinner party introduces a range of characters who will help to expand the concerns of the novel. The relationship between Tipton Grange and Middlemarch is indicated, and Lydgate's story is linked to that of Dorothea.

Fuller Thomas Fuller (1608–81), clergyman and author
De Quincey's Thomas De Quincey (1785–1859), essayist
an immortal physicist Thomas Young (1773–1829), physicist and Egyptologist
Tartarean shades Tartarus was the underworld in Greek myth. Shades connotes both shadows and spirits
Santa Barbara an early Christian saint, whose father imprisoned her to preserve her beauty
Broussais François Broussais (1772–1838), French surgeon and physician

CHAPTER 11   **Rosamond and Fred Vincy, at home with their mother. Fred, who anticipates a legacy from his uncle Featherstone, speaks of Lydgate**

Lydgate has become fascinated by Rosamond Vincy, who is now introduced. Sitting with her mother, working at embroidery, she is clearly bored. Her brother Fred comes down late to breakfast, and speaks of Lydgate, who has been attending their ailing uncle, Mr Featherstone. Fred evidently anticipates an inheritance from the old man. Rosamond objects to her uncle's cough and 'his ugly relations' (p. 101). They discuss

Mary Garth, a niece of Featherstone's first wife, who is looking after him. Mrs Vincy exhorts her son to study in order to take his degree. After making plans to ride next morning to Stone Court, Featherstone's home, Fred and Rosamond play music together.

It is clear that Lydgate is as steeped in patriarchal assumptions as Mr Brooke and Mr Chichely. He believes that a woman 'ought to produce the effect of exquisite music' (p. 94), and considers that a wife should be an adornment.

The narrator surveys changes occurring within provincial society, modifying the composition of the town and the parish, and altering the relationships between them. Within this context, significant differences between Rosamond and Fred are evident. Rosamond is obsessed with class. This is evident from their discussion of language, but also in her view of Lydgate. She is attracted by his good breeding. Her emphasis resembles that of her mother, whose snobbishness is evident in her view of Mary Garth and her family.

Mr Vincy is mayor, but also a manufacturer, of the kind looked down upon by Mrs Cadwallader. Fred, like his father, recognises that money is becoming more important than the old class distinctions. He points out that in financial terms Tertius Lydgate is a poor branch on the family tree.

Ben Jonson (1572–1637), poet and dramatist

the solar guinea gold coin, minted until 1813

Herodotus (*c*.480–*c*.425BC), Greek historian

Ar hyd y nos (Welsh song) 'All through the night'

CHAPTER 12   **Fred and Rosamond visit Featherstone. He is attended by Mary Garth, whom Fred hopes to marry. Featherstone requires his nephew to secure a letter from Bulstrode clearing him of borrowing money on the strength of the anticipated inheritance. Lydgate is struck by Rosamond's appearance**

Fred and Rosamond Vincy ride to Stone Court, home of Peter Featherstone, whose death is thought to be imminent. Mrs Waule, formerly Jane Featherstone, is with her brother. She speaks of Fred's habitual gambling at billiards. Rosamond arrives, and Featherstone dismisses his sister from their company. Fred arrives, after attending to the horses, and Featherstone speaks with him alone, while Rosamond talks with Mary Garth in Mary's room.

The old man accuses Fred of borrowing money on the strength of an anticipated inheritance from him. The accusation is unjustified, although Fred has spoken of that prospect as a means to settle future debts. The allegation originated with Mr Bulstrode, and Featherstone requests that Fred obtains a letter from the banker clearing his name. Fred, aware that the pious Bulstrode dislikes him, is horrified.

Rosamond discusses Lydgate with Mary. Then, she sings for Featherstone. Lydgate arrives. The Vincys soon depart, but the doctor is struck by Rosamond's beauty, and she is attracted to him.

On the way home, Fred is troubled by his uncle's request. He decides to ask his father to speak with Bulstrode on his behalf. Rosamond tells him that Mary Garth has said she would not accept an offer of marriage from Fred.

Mrs Waule attempts to discredit Fred Vincy in order to enhance her own prospects of inheritance from her brother. Such devious selfishness appears reprehensible, but self-interest takes many forms in *Middlemarch*, and it is not always so easy to criticise. For example, Dorothea is drawn to Casaubon because she hopes he will open the door to knowledge for her. He marries her so she can assist with his work. Rosamond sees Lydgate as the means to elevate her own social position, and like Dorothea, she senses that she is entering 'the great epoch of her life' (p. 118). Lydgate is attracted to her as a decorative adornment.

The love between Fred and Mary, on the other hand, seems to be against the self-interest of either. Fred shows no promise that he will be a reliable husband; Mary is considered plain, (especially when compared to Rosamond), and is from a lower social class. Their relationship takes a long time to blossom, but it is rooted in genuine friendship. That is a recipe for success which most other couples portrayed here do not possess, although it can be seen to underpin the marriage of Mary's parents, and of the Cadwalladers.

an articulated pupil a pupil who takes on some teaching duties, while receiving an education

Josephus Flavius Josephus (37–100), Jewish historian

Culpepper Sir Thomas Culpepper, seventeenth-century writer on usury

Klopstock's *Messiah* Friedrich Klopstock, German poet whose *Messiah* (1773) was a religious epic written in imitation of Milton

the Gentleman's magazine conservative periodical founded in 1731

il y en a pour tous les goûts (French) there is something for all tastes

old Overreach Sir Giles Overreach, villain in Philip Massinger's play, *A New Way to Pay Old Debts* (1633)

Book two: old and young

CHAPTER 13   Mr Vincy visits Mr Bulstrode, seeking a letter clearing his son of financial impropriety

Mr Vincy visits Bulstrode's office. He has to wait while the banker talks with Lydgate. Bulstrode has been entrusted with overseeing the development of the new fever hospital. He asks the doctor to support the candidacy of Mr Tyke, rather than Mr Farebrother, to become hospital chaplain. Lydgate admits that his interest lies with physical rather than spiritual welfare.

After Lydgate's departure, Vincy and Bulstrode discuss Fred, and Featherstone's challenge to him. Bulstrode refuses to co-operate, expressing pious disapproval of the manner of Fred's upbringing. Vincy loses his temper. Bulstrode then says he will consult his wife, Vincy's sister, and will send a letter.

Bulstrode feels an affinity with Lydgate as a stranger in Middlemarch. The banker is a powerful man, but he has not really been accepted by the community. Strong religious convictions feed his zeal in supporting the new hospital. Lydgate, on the other hand, is concerned to elevate the reputation of his profession by improving its practices. He sees the fever hospital not merely as of immediate practical use, but as the potential centre for a medical school. He shares the reforming spirit of the times, yet exhibits a dogged commitment to his work, comparable to that shown by Casaubon.

In Chapter 15 we are told that Lydgate regards the medical profession as 'the most direct alliance between intellectual conquest and the social good' (p. 145). In his plan 'to do good small work for Middlemarch, and great work for the world' (p. 149) he combines Dorothea's compassionate local concerns and her husband's grander conception.

CHAPTER 14   **Fred Vincy takes the letter from Bulstrode to Featherstone, and is given one hundred pounds. Mary Garth tells him she will not marry an idle man who incurs debts**

A letter arrives carrying the requested testimony from Bulstrode. Fred takes it to Featherstone. The old man attempts to humiliate Fred, but eventually gives him one hundred pounds. This falls short of the amount required to settle his debts. Fred burns the letter, and is relieved to be able to depart when Simmons, a bailiff, arrives to discuss the old man's farm. Mary Garth tells Fred she would not marry an idle debtor. He lodges eighty pounds with his mother towards payment of the one hundred and sixty pounds he owes. Mary's father has acted as signatory towards security for the debt.

Fred laments that 'a woman is never in love with any one she has always known – ever since she can remember; as a man often is. It is always some new fellow who strikes a girl' (p. 138). We are reminded here of Lydgate's allure for Rosamond – certainly enhanced by him being a newcomer. In fact, Mary reciprocates Fred's feelings, developed over the years, and, although it is concealed for much of the novel, there is an enduring strength in their relationship.

Brenda Troil Brenda and Minna Troil, Merton, and Cleveland are characters in Walter Scott's novel *The Pirate* (1822)

Waverley Waverley and Flora MacIvor are characters in Scott's *Waverley* (1814)

Olivia and Sophia Primrose characters in Oliver Goldsmith's *The Vicar of Wakefield* (1766)

Corinne eponymous heroine of a novel by Madame de Staël (1807)

CHAPTER 15   Lydgate's character, his background, and his
               aspirations

The state of medicine in 1829 is considered. Lydgate, who is a focus for imaginative speculation amongst local people, is reputed more clever than most doctors. There is an account of his past and description of his character. He is concerned to add to medical knowledge, to advance the profession and reform its practice. The story of his youthful romance in Paris is told. He proposed marriage to an actress, but was horrified to discover that she had deliberately murdered her husband on stage, while performing a melodrama.

> The complex plot of *Middlemarch* should not distract us from consideration of the narrative voice. Here the narrator muses on the tendency of novelist Henry Fielding (1707–54) to make interventions, introducing personal comments and digressions. It is suggested that Fielding lived in a more relaxed age; there is no longer time for such a leisurely approach.
>
> Fielding's voice passed authoritative moral judgements in his novels. For George Eliot the world was no longer so clear-cut, and her narrative voice is altogether more complex. Remember that George Eliot was the male pseudonym of a woman writer. If we allow ourselves to identify narrator and author, is it a man's voice, or a woman's? Fred Vincy has remarked, 'All choice of words is slang. It marks a class' (p. 99). Does vocabulary enable us to determine the class to which the narrator belongs? More fundamentally, is the voice consistent, or does it change in order to reflect varying points of view? (See Narrative Technique.)
>
> Lydgate is driven by concern for his profession, but also by the spirit of adventure. Pathology is compared to America, which in 1829 offered extensive opportunities for exploration of uncharted territory. The melodramatic tale of Lydgate's Parisian infatuation starkly contrasts with the narrowly provincial propriety of Middlemarch. It discloses a passionate element within Lydgate's character, which seems now to have become largely subordinated to the demands of his work.

Lydgate's intellectual hero is the French physiologist Bichat. Bichat considered tissues 'ultimate facts in the living organism, marking the limit of anatomical analysis'. Lydgate aspires to advance beyond this position, and to discover the 'primitive tissue' from which all others are derived (p. 148). His research offers a clear parallel to that of Casaubon, who seeks the key to mythologies. One man works with myth, the other with science, but neither attains their goal. George Eliot seems to suggest that the desire to discover points of origin and keys to total knowledge was no longer tenable in the late nineteenth century (see Historical Background: Loss of faith).

Bichat held that living organisms had to be regarded as 'consisting of certain primary webs or tissues' (p. 148). This scientific belief offers a **metaphor** for the view of human life presented in *Middlemarch*. No character can be viewed in isolation; individuals are caught up in webs of relationships with others, and it is these relationships, rather than personal desires, that tend to determine their fate.

Rasselas *Rasselas* (1759), fictional work by Samuel Johnson (1709–84)

Gulliver *Gulliver's Travels* (1726), satirical work by Jonathan Swift (1667–1745)

Bailey's Dictionary Nathan Bailey's *A Universal Etymological Dictionary* (1721)

Chrysal, or the Adventures of a Guinea satirical work by Charles Johnstone, published 1760–5

makdom and her fairnesse form and beauty

Jenner Edward Jenner (1749–1823), pioneer of vaccination

Herschel Sir William Herschel (1738–1822), astronomer

a recent legal decision a case enforcing the Apothecaries Act (1815), which insisted that dispensing chemists should be suitably qualified

Bichat Marie François Bichat (1771–1802), pioneering anatomist and physiologist

Saint-Simonians followers of the Utopian socialist, Comte de Saint-Simon (1760–1825)

Offenbach Jacques Offenbach (1819–80), composer

CHAPTER 16   A dinner party at Mr Vincy's. The contest between
Farebrother and Tyke to become chaplain to the New
Hospital is discussed. The conversation shifts to the
attractiveness of Rosamond Vincy, who entertains
the company with her piano-playing. Afterwards,
Lydgate returns home to his medical studies

Lydgate attends Mr Vincy's dinner party. Mr Chichely the coroner, and
Dr Sprague, the town's senior surgeon, are also present. Tyke's candidacy
to be salaried chaplain to the hospital is discussed. Lydgate recognises
the social power exercised by Bulstrode. The mayor favours the
companionable Farebrother against the drily doctrinaire Tyke. Lydgate
says his choice will be made according to the prospects for reform.
Mention of reform unsettles the older men.

In the drawing-room, Chichely notes jealously the animation with
which Rosamond talks to the young doctor. Lydgate is enchanted when
she plays the piano.

Mr Farebrother arrives. He plays whist, and Lydgate observes
in him 'a striking mixture of the shrewd and the mild' (p. 167). Returning
home, Lydgate weighs the merits of Farebrother against his own
need for the influential Bulstrode's support. Rosamond is a secondary
consideration to him at this point.

At home, he immerses himself in medical study. He is pleased to
have chosen a profession that requires 'the highest intellectual strain'
while keeping him 'in good warm contact with his neighbours' (p. 165).

In contrast to the altruism of Dorothea and Lydgate, Bulstrode
indulges, like old Featherstone, in 'a sort of vampire's feast in the
sense of mastery' (p. 156): despite his overt piety, the banker is
perceived as a man who derives pleasure from exercising control
over others.

The good humour of the Vincy household is noted, and Lydgate
recognises it. Nonetheless, he views such evenings as 'a wretched
waste' (p. 162). Like Casaubon, he considers social life an
impediment to the serious business of his work. That attitude
bodes no better for his relationship with Rosamond than it did
for Casaubon's with Dorothea.

Lydgate admires Rosamond because she is 'polished, refined, docile' (p. 164). The concluding adjective discloses his requirement of obedience from a woman. Once they are married, Lydgate will discover that Rosamond is by no means 'docile'. The narrator does not conceal the immense distance separating their points of view: 'Poor Lydgate! or shall I say, Poor Rosamond! Each lived in a world of which the other knew nothing' (p. 165).

Wakley Thomas Wakley (1795–1862), founder in 1823 of the medical journal *The Lancet*

prick-eared priggish. The term derives from the close-cropped hair of Oliver Cromwell's followers

Haydn's canzonets songs by Josef Haydn (1732–1809)

'Voi, che sapete', or 'Batti, batti' quotations from Mozart's operas *The Marriage of Figaro* and *Don Giovanni*

Niobe in Greek myth, a boastful mother, turned to stone by Apollo and Artemis

Louis Pierre Louis (1781–1872), French authority on typhoid

Lalla Rookh narrative poem by Thomas Moore, published in 1817

CHAPTER 17 **Lydgate visits Farebrother's parsonage and meets his family**

Lydgate visits Farebrother's parsonage, and meets his elder sister Winifred, their mother, and her sister, Miss Noble. After tea the two men retire to the parson's study. Farebrother refers to the factionalism in Middlemarch life, and mentions Bulstrode's hostility to him. Lydgate defends the banker's good ideas, deeds, and intentions. Farebrother says he will value Lydgate's friendship even if the doctor feels compelled to vote against him.

Mrs Farebrother is disparaging of pretentious sermons when she says: 'When you get me a good man made out of arguments, I will get you a good dinner with reading you the cookery-book' (p. 170). But her point can be applied equally to the work undertaken by both Casaubon and Lydgate. In neither case does their research enable them to live more successfully with others. Lydgate is investigating the human body as a web of relationships, but he is unable to recognise the comparable web which binds individuals within the body of society. His judgement is accordingly blinkered, as he sustains a naive view of his own independence.

The warm portrayal of Farebrother's family prepares us to favour him over the zealously doctrinaire Tyke. Their names illustrate well the artifice George Eliot employs to guide our reading. The sound of Farebrother suggests fairness and fraternity, while the pugnacious word Tyke denotes an obstinate boor. Farebrother's considerate and tolerant character is summed up in his declaration, 'I don't translate my own convenience into other people's duties' (p. 175). He refuses to impose on other people his own point of view.

aphis brassicae   garden pest that feeds on cabbages
Philomicron   (Greek) lover of small things
Pythagorean community   Utopian community of the kind formed by the Greek philosopher Pythagoras in the sixth century BC
Robert Brown   (1773–1853), botanist
amour-propre   (French) vanity

CHAPTER 18   **The vote for the chaplaincy takes place. Lydgate, who has the deciding vote, supports Tyke**

Some weeks later, the election to the chaplaincy takes place. In the interim, Lydgate has come to like Farebrother more and more, and he remains uncertain how to vote.

At the hospital, Dr Sprague, the other surgeons, and some of the directors have assembled. Sprague and Minchin both resent Bulstrode's intervention into Middlemarch life. Wrench and Toller disparage Lydgate as Bulstrode's lackey.

Frank Hawley, lawyer and town-clerk, points out that Farebrother has been doing the work without pay, and should now be remunerated for his efforts. The vote takes place. The casting-vote falls to Lydgate. He sides with Tyke, who consequently becomes Chaplain to the Infirmary. Lydgate is uneasy about his decision.

This meeting is the crucial occasion where Lydgate begins to realise that he cannot act according to 'his unmixed resolutions of independence and his select purpose'. Here he feels 'the hampering threadlike pressure of small social conditions, and their frustrating complexity' (p. 180). He is being shaped within the web of Middlemarch life.

Pope's *Essay on Man* poem published in 1733 by Alexander Pope (1688–1744)
Prodicus author in the fifth century BC of 'The Choice of Hercules'
the Nessus shirt garment soaked in the poisoned blood of the centaur Nessus, which killed Hercules when he wore it

CHAPTER 19 Ladislaw, with his friend Naumann, sees Dorothea in the Vatican gallery

In the Vatican gallery, in Rome, Will Ladislaw and his friend, Adolf Naumann, a young German artist, observe Dorothea. Despite the fact that she is 'clad in Quakerish grey drapery' (p. 189), Naumann admires her, taking special note of her beautiful hands. Ladislaw, clearly ruffled, identifies her as the wife of his second-cousin. Naumann, who wants Dorothea to model for a painting, perceives that Ladislaw is jealous of Casaubon.

The scene shifts from Middlemarch to Rome. Dorothea's chaste clothing looks even more out of place amid the richness of this city. Ladislaw is accustomed to European travel. His cosmopolitan outlook contrasts with the narrow provincialism of Dorothea's upbringing. His friendship with a German artist confirms his affinity with **Romantic** aesthetics and philosophy. His knowledge of contemporary German culture allows him a perspective upon Casaubon's work which will soon prove revelatory and shocking to Dorothea.

Purgatorio vii 'See the other, who, sighing, has made a bed for her cheek with the palm of her hand'
the most brilliant English critic of his day William Hazlitt (1778–1830), essayist
certain long-haired German artists at Rome reference to a group known as the Nazarenes
Meleager hunter in Greek mythology

Ariadne daughter of King Minos of Crete. She used a ball of thread to assist the escape of Theseus from the labyrinth, after he had killed the Minotaur

Geistlicher **(German)** clergyman

Antigone in Greek myth, the daughter of Oedipus. A model of filial devotion

Der Neffe als Onkel comedy by the German dramatist Schiller (1803)

ungeheuer (German) monstrous

CHAPTER 20   **Dorothea feels neglected by her husband. She offers to assist with his work, but her remarks anger him**

Dorothea offers to assist preparation of a text for publication from her husband's copious notes. Casaubon responds with anger to her comments regarding the inconclusive state of his work, and Dorothea becomes indignant in turn. She tries to effect reconciliation, and goes with him to the Vatican. It is after Casaubon has left her for the library that Naumann first observes her, as recorded in the previous chapter.

Two hours later, Dorothea sits sobbing in her room. She has been in Rome for five weeks. Casaubon has buried himself in study at the Vatican library, and his young wife from provincial Middlemarch feels isolated in the strange old city. Her perception of marriage to Casaubon has undergone dramatic revision.

> Dorothea's discontent grows as the 'stupendous fragmentariness of the ancient city heightens the dreamlike strangeness of her bridal life' (p. 192). She feels out of place amongst Rome's 'ruins and basilicas, palaces and colossi' (p. 193). The landscape and architecture suggest a **metaphor** appropriate to describe her changing perception of Casaubon: 'the large vistas and wide fresh air which she had dreamed of finding in her husband's mind were replaced by ante-rooms and winding passages which seemed to lead nowhither' (p. 195).
>
> This chapter contains a sequence comparable to cinematic **flashback**, recounting earlier events in order to cast light on the circumstances which resulted in Dorothea's presence at the Vatican gallery.

Cabeiri Samothracian fertility gods

CHAPTER 21   **Ladislaw visits Dorothea in her apartment. He**
recognises that she has been weeping. They discuss
Casaubon's work. Casaubon returns from his studies

Dorothea stops sobbing when Tantripp, her maid, announces the arrival
of a gentleman, related to Casaubon, who wishes to see her. Ladislaw
reveals that he saw her earlier in the Vatican museum. He recognises that
she has been weeping, and feels appalled at the thought of Casaubon
spending his honeymoon 'groping after his mouldy futilities' (p. 205). He
talks of painting, and then discusses her husband's work, suggesting that
new scholarship in Germany has rendered those labours obsolete.
Casaubon arrives home and, making it clear he is too tired for company,
invites Ladislaw to dinner the following day.

> The circumstances of Dorothea's honeymoon lead Ladislaw to feel
> 'a sort of comic disgust' (p. 205). The word 'disgust' links his
> reaction to those of Celia and Chettam upon learning of the
> engagement.

CHAPTER 22   **Ladislaw dines with Mr and Mrs Casaubon. The**
following day he conducts them around artists'
studios. Naumann sketches the couple. The next day,
Ladislaw visits Dorothea when she is alone, and
laments the conditions of her marriage. He affirms
that Casaubon's scholarship is outmoded and
determines to live independently of his cousin

Casaubon and Dorothea find Ladislaw an agreeable dinner guest, and it
is agreed that he will conduct them to artists' studios the following day.
They visit Naumann, and Ladislaw shows them some of his own
sketches. Naumann asks Casaubon to sit for him, as his head will be
perfect for his painting of St Thomas Aquinas. He seizes the opportunity
to sketch Dorothea, in the pose of Santa Clara.

Left alone, the two young men mock Casaubon's self-centredness,
and extol the beauty of his wife. Ladislaw desires to see Dorothea
alone, in order to make a more emphatic impression on her. He visits
around noon the following day, when her husband is out. Dorothea is
choosing cameo jewellery for Celia. Ladislaw speaks with passion against

Dorothea's cloistered life. She asserts that Lowick Manor is her chosen home.

She presses him on the shortcomings in Casaubon's work, when compared to that of German scholars. Ladislaw's remarks make her angry, and he announces his intention to return to England and live independently of Casaubon's financial support. He declares he will not see Dorothea again. They speak with evident warmth for one another, and tears appear in their eyes.

Departing, Ladislaw encounters Casaubon and they exchange farewells. That evening Dorothea tells her husband of Ladislaw's resolve to live independently. Casaubon responds with cold disinterest. He asks Dorothea to desist from further mention of Ladislaw.

In the early days of their acquaintance, Dorothea frequently compared Casaubon to eminent men such as Locke, Milton, and Pascal. She is delighted when Naumann asks her husband to act as a model for his portrait of Aquinas. Neither she nor her husband recognises the mockery of the invitation, which is really an excuse for the artist to spend time in Dorothea's company. It is characteristic of Casaubon's self-centredness that he arranges to buy the flattering portrait of himself, but shows little interest in the depiction of his wife.

Ladislaw remarks that scholarship in Casaubon's field is 'as changing as chemistry: new discoveries are constantly making new points of view' (p. 222). George Eliot was acutely aware of changes wrought in all fields of knowledge as the nineteenth century unfolded. Ladislaw identifies a process which was to result in widespread anxiety in European culture as old and comforting certainties gave way to new and unfamiliar interpretations.

Middleton Conyers Middleton (1682–1750), theological controversialist

the Madonna di Foligno painting by Raphael

the Laocoon statue in the Vatican museum

Thorwaldsen Bertel Thorwaldsen (1770–1844), Danish sculptor based in Rome

pfuscherei (German) bungling

Minotaurs in Greek myth, the minotaur had the head of a bull and the body of a man

Paracelsus pseudonym of Theophrastus Bombastus von Hohenheim (1493–1541), Swiss physician

Bryant Jacob Bryant (1715–1804), author of *An Analysis of Ancient Mythology*

Cush and Mizraim sons of Ham, who was son of Noah

porte cochère (French) carriage entrance

BOOK THREE: WAITING FOR DEATH

CHAPTER 23   **On account of his debts, Fred Vincy decides to sell his horse to raise cash, but buys another at greater expense**

Fred Vincy owes one hundred and sixty pounds to Bambridge, a local horse-dealer. Fred is optimistic about prospects for settling the debt, for which Caleb Garth has acted as security. Mrs Vincy fears an engagement between her son and Mary Garth, who have been close friends since childhood.

Featherstone's gift of £100 fell short of Fred's immediate financial requirements, and he determines to sell his horse in order to raise money. After retrieving the eighty pounds entrusted to his mother, Fred rides to Houndsley horse-fair. On the way, at the Red Lion inn, Fred exchanges his horse plus thirty pounds for a grey horse called Diamond, which he hopes to sell to Lord Medlicote for eighty pounds.

Debt is an important factor in the plot of *Middlemarch*. Financial debts are a clear measure of dependency upon others. Fred endures the humiliation administered by Featherstone because he hopes to inherit money from him. On the other hand, his unsettled debts will have repercussions for the kindly Garth family. Lydgate develops substantial debts later in the novel, and as a consequence becomes entangled with Bulstrode's fate. Economic relationships of this kind illustrate that nobody lives in isolation, and that individual characters are inevitably caught up in a web of dependencies and responsibilities.

Lindley Murray author of *English Grammar* (1795)

Mangnall's *Questions* Mrs Richmal Mangnall's *Historical and Miscellaneous Questions* (1800), a standard school textbook

jockies horse-dealers
blacklegs swindlers at horse-racing
roarer horse that breathes heavily
sawyers timber-yard workers

CHAPTER 24   **Fred's new horse injures itself. He admits to Caleb Garth that he is unable to pay his debts. Money set aside for the education of Garth's son Alfred will be used for that purpose**

The horse, Diamond, proves to be wild and injures itself. The debt has to be settled soon, and Fred has only fifty pounds left. He rides to the Garth family's old-fashioned, rambling house, and finds Mrs Garth doing housework, while providing education for her children, Letty and Ben. She tells Fred that she has only one other pupil at present to add to her income.

Caleb Garth arrives home. Fred reveals his financial plight. Mrs Garth was previously unaware of her husband's involvement with the debt. He is too short of money to help, but his wife offers savings reserved for their son Alfred's education. Mary will be able to provide the remainder.

Her kindness touches Fred with remorse. He departs feeling extremely uncomfortable. Susan Garth expresses her disappointment with Fred, and agrees with her husband's view that he himself has acted foolishly. She tells him to desist from his habit of working without payment.

Education is another major concern in *Middlemarch*. George Eliot does not idealise learning: Casaubon's erudition proves sterile; Lydgate experiences serious problems despite his specialist knowledge. Nonetheless, education clearly plays its part in the author's conception of the general development of society. Women in nineteenth-century England were denied access to educational opportunities open to men, and that is reflected in the very different experiences of Dorothea and of Rosamond.

Mrs Garth, who is presented throughout as an admirable woman, teaches her own children and takes in pupils to supplement the family's income. Her learning extends, however, only to the fundamentals of education, and she unquestioningly endorses the view that women are 'framed to be entirely subordinate' (p. 243). She accepts that men are socially superior. Her son Christy is at university, and it was intended that his brother Alfred should follow him. But she is content for her daughter Mary to act as a servant to Featherstone (see Themes: Gender).

the Subjunctive Mood in grammar, the mode of verbs in sentences expressing uncertainty
the Torrid Zone region of the earth between the tropics

CHAPTER 25   **Fred reveals to Mary Garth the position in which he has placed her parents. She is furious. Fred leaves, feeling ill. Garth visits his daughter to borrow money from her**

Fred rides to Stone Court and tells Mary of his debt, and of the position in which her father has been placed. Mary cries, furious that her parents should now face such difficulties. Despite her anger, she manages to feel pity for Fred. After paying a short visit to Featherstone, Fred departs, feeling unwell.

Soon after dusk, Caleb Garth arrives at Stone Court. After brief discussion with Featherstone, he talks with Mary about his obligation to settle the debt. Garth advises his daughter not to become entangled in Fred's future. Mary assures him, 'I will never engage myself to one who has no manly independence, and who goes on loitering away his time on the chance that others will provide for him' (p. 257). Taking eighteen pounds from her, Garth leaves Mary alone with Featherstone.

Mary Garth does not have the beauty of Rosamond, nor the aspirations of Dorothea. She is plain, and she applies herself to practical tasks with exemplary common sense. But, perhaps because she lacks physical attractiveness and intellectual ambition, she has a rare capacity for sympathy, which is evident even here, when Fred has wronged her family. In a novel peopled with characters who are blinkered by selfishness, Mary's altruism provides a telling contrast (see Themes: Altruism and Egotism).

Mary is not an idealised character, however. One of her failings, which she has in common with her mother, is a ready acceptance of female subordination. She makes 'manly independence' a criterion for an acceptable husband, and chides Fred for his complacency. But independence is never so straightforward, as *Middlemarch* persistently shows.

Mrs Piozzi's recollections of Johnson Hester Lynch Piozzi published *Anecdotes of the late Samuel Johnson*, in 1786

CHAPTER 26   Fred's illness intensifies. Lydgate attends him, and diagnoses typhoid

Fred feels unwell, and asks his mother to send for Mr Wrench. The doctor assures them the illness is not serious. The next morning the fever, contracted in the unsanitary streets of Houndsley, has intensified. Rosamond notices Lydgate passing their house, and her mother asks for his help. Lydgate diagnoses typhoid and prescribes a suitable course of treatment.

This chapter presents a dramatic rendering of the conflict between old and new medical practices, as exemplified by Wrench and Lydgate. George Eliot's historical perspective when writing the novel allowed even initial readers to recognise that Lydgate's 'new' approach had eventually proved successful. But within the novel Lydgate's reforming zeal achieves very little in practical terms. George Eliot is showing that change has to overcome resistance, and is invariably achieved through gradual evolution.

CHAPTER 27   Fred's health steadily improves. Romance develops between Rosamond and Lydgate

The younger Vincys are sent away on account of Fred's illness. Rosamond remains with her parents, and she and Lydgate are brought 'within effective proximity' (p. 264). As Fred steadily improves, a message from Featherstone arrives, announcing that the old man has missed his visits. Fred is upset not to have heard from Mary.

The 'mutual fascination' (p. 266) between Lydgate and Rosamond persists after normality has been restored to the house. Lydgate, who lacks money and is dedicated to research, does not intend to marry for several years. Rosamond, on the other hand, eagerly anticipates their marriage, and 'a handsome house' (p. 267). Lydgate's evident success with Rosamond arouses hostility amongst rivals for her affection, including Ned Plymdale. Lydgate is summoned to attend at Lowick Manor.

> *Middlemarch* is subtitled 'A Study of Provincial Life', and the narrowness of experience this implies is one of the novel's major concerns. Limited horizons breed false expectations; this is the case with Rosamond's view of Lydgate, as it is with Dorothea's view of Casaubon. In both relationships the young women anticipate that marriage will grant access to a new and fulfilling world.

> Lydgate's relative urbanity is emphasised through contrast with the provincial outlook of Rosamond's other suitor, Ned Plymdale. It is ironic that while Rosamond's romantic involvement with the doctor develops, Fred feels helplessly isolated from the contentedly provincial woman he loves, Mary Garth.

> The summons to Lowick Manor indicates Lydgate's growing reputation. It also signals convergence between the two main strands of the story. The circumstances which resulted in the summons are described in Chapter 29.

> **Keepsake** fashionable literary annual
> **Lady Blessington** Lady Blessington (1789–1849), novelist who edited *The Keepsake*
> **and L.E.L.** Letitia Elizabeth Landon (1803–38), poet and novelist

CHAPTER 28   **The Casaubons return home. Mr Casaubon is unwell**

The Casaubons return to Lowick Manor in mid-January. Casaubon gets up early, complaining of heart palpitations. Later, Celia and her uncle arrive. Brooke notes Casaubon's paleness. Celia tells Dorothea of her engagement to Sir James Chettam.

> Middlemarch's provincial nature is again highlighted here. Following her exposure to the wider world, Lowick seems altogether less consequential to Dorothea. Her expectation of

active involvement in her husband's intellectual endeavours has also diminished. She now inhabits 'a pale fantastic world that seemed to be vanishing from the daylight' (p. 274). She remains ardent in her desire for a more fulfilling life, but her existence seems to have become 'a nightmare in which every object was withering and shrinking away from her' (p. 275).

The portrait of Casaubon's aunt Julia starts to exercise a strange fascination for Dorothea, explicable in part because she is said to have made an unfortunate marriage, but also because this woman was the grandmother of Will Ladislaw, the young man who has awakened Dorothea's emotional life. Meanwhile, her devoted attention to Casaubon has waned to the point where others recognise in her husband 'signs which she had not noticed' (p. 276).

CHAPTER 29   **A letter from Ladislaw annoys Casaubon who, soon afterwards, suffers a heart-attack. Lydgate attends to him**

Several weeks later, Dorothea joins her husband in the library, where he is at work. Casaubon gives her a letter from Ladislaw. It was enclosed with another, addressed to him, in which Ladislaw proposed that he should visit Lowick. Casaubon intends to decline that proposal on the grounds that he is too busy to be distracted by the younger man's 'desultory vivacity' (p. 282). Dorothea reacts angrily, and turns resentfully to the copying work Casaubon has allocated to her, leaving the letter from Ladislaw unread.

After half an hour, she is startled by the sound of a book falling and finds Casaubon in physical distress, struggling to breathe. She assists him with tender concern. Arriving to discover Casaubon lying on a couch, slowly reviving, and Dorothea recovering from her shock, Chettam recommends that they send for Lydgate. The doctor soon comes, and attends to the couple. Chettam and Celia lament Dorothea's marriage to Casaubon.

The narrator insists that we should try to consider matters from Casaubon's point of view, despite the fact that he lacks the personal charms so evident in his young wife. The narrator actually affirms,

'For my part I am very sorry for him' (p. 280). Again we might ask, whose voice is this? Is this declaration of fellow-feeling consistent with the general presentation of Casaubon in the narrative?

George Eliot is involving us directly with two of the novel's main concerns: point of view, and the capacity to extend sympathy to others. At the same time, it is evident that the points of view of Casaubon and Dorothea are growing further apart, and that the capacity for sympathy between them is accordingly diminished. Moreover, despite Casaubon's illness he is not regarded sympathetically by Celia, who says she 'never did like him', nor by Chettam, who considers the marriage 'a horrible sacrifice' of Dorothea (p. 284).

The arrival of Lydgate to attend to Casaubon is continuous with the end of Chapter 27.

Parerga secondary works

Brasenose college of Oxford University

Warburton's William Warburton (1698–1779), bishop

viros nullo aevo perituros (Latin) men who will never pass away

CHAPTER 30   **Lydgate alerts Dorothea to the possibility that her husband might die suddenly. She asks her uncle to deter a visit from Ladislaw, but Brooke invites the young man to call on him at Tipton Grange**

It is March. Immediate danger has passed, but Lydgate continues to attend to Casaubon. He advises that his patient should work less. Lydgate tells Dorothea that Casaubon is almost restored to his usual state of health, but recommends watchfulness. He says her husband might live fifteen years or more. On the other hand, death might occur suddenly. Casaubon should be kept as free from anxiety as possible.

Dorothea is outwardly calm but turbulent inside. Once alone, she cries. Composing herself, she reads Ladislaw's letters. He intends to make his way in life independently. At a convenient time, he will visit Lowick to deliver Naumann's picture, featuring Casaubon as Aquinas.

She asks her uncle to contact Ladislaw, informing him that Casaubon's illness precludes such a visit. In the course of writing, however, Brooke invites Ladislaw to visit him at Tipton Grange. He envisages that Ladislaw's talents might assist his own political ambition.

Dorothea asks Lydgate for help. We are told that the request stayed with him for years, a 'cry from soul to soul, without other consciousness than their moving with kindred natures in the same embroiled medium, the same troublous fitfully-illuminated life' (p. 290). This elevated description conveys the high seriousness with which both characters view the world and their role in it. It confirms that they are to be seen as parallel figures, sharing high aspirations and meeting with bitter disappointments.

Smollett Tobias Smollett (1721–1771), Scottish novelist

CHAPTER 31   Fred Vincy recuperates at Stone Court. Lydgate and Rosamond are engaged

In order to recuperate, Fred Vincy stays for a while at Stone Court. His mother goes with him, eager to prevent an engagement to Mary Garth. Mrs Bulstrode pays regular visits to her brother, in his wife's absence. Ned Plymdale's mother has alerted her to the intimacy growing between Rosamond and Lydgate. She challenges her niece directly. Rosamond denies entering into a secret engagement. Her aunt cautions that Lydgate is poor. Rosamond responds with reference to the doctor's good family connections. Mrs Bulstrode speaks favourably of Ned Plymdale as a potential husband.

Mr Bulstrode is pressed by his wife to inquire after Lydgate's intentions. The doctor declares he has no intention of marrying. Mrs Bulstrode then speaks directly with Lydgate. The doctor is disturbed by this intrusion into his affairs, and resolves to visit the Vincys only when business necessitates.

Visiting Stone Court, Lydgate is asked by Mrs Vincy to report to her husband a decline in Featherstone's health, and to request that he visit the old man. Lydgate finds Rosamond alone. Both are embarrassed, and his forced formality upsets her. She cries; he holds and kisses her. They become engaged. Lydgate returns that evening to gain her father's approval. Vincy, aware of the imminent demise of Featherstone, is buoyant at the prospect of Fred's likely inheritance, and he grants assent without hesitation.

Lydgate's declaration that he prefers to tend the poor rather than the wealthy indicates his selfless dedication to the profession of medicine, untainted by material considerations. It does not bode well for his marriage to the materialistic Rosamond.

We are told that Rosamond has 'a great sense of being a romantic heroine, and playing the part prettily' (p. 297). This not only suggests her superficiality, but also recalls the actress with whom Lydgate was infatuated in Paris, and who killed her own husband. George Eliot avoids presenting Rosamond as a villain, however; rather, she is a victim of narrow horizons imposed by patriarchal assumptions. She has been made vain and shallow by her education and her stereotypical femininity.

sirens enchantresses in Greek myth, whose singing lured sailors to their death

Ariadne Theseus deserted Ariadne after she had led him from the labyrinth

CHAPTER 32   Featherstone's relatives gather as his health deteriorates

Featherstone's blood relations are agitated at the prospect of his imminent demise. They become intensely watchful of one another, and of other possible claimants. The old man refuses to see these visitors. Some linger in the kitchen, where Mary Garth finds herself under constant scrutiny.

Featherstone's brother Solomon, and his sister, Jane Waule, suspect that their brother has left money to Mary. They are outraged to find Mrs Vincy and Fred in the old man's company, while they are rebuffed. The auctioneer, Borthrop Trumbull, who is to be a bearer at the funeral, is also allowed to visit the old man.

Featherstone's relatives appear comically grotesque in their self-centredness, but their greed, envy, and lack of sympathy for the dying man are really just extreme depictions of qualities exhibited by more central figures in the novel. At the start of Chapter 31, for example, Rosamond remarks that Dorothea is 'of course' devoted to Casaubon, 'but she was thinking at the same time that it was not so very melancholy to be mistress of Lowick Manor with a husband likely to die soon' (p. 293).

Brobdingnag land of giants in Jonathan Swift's *Gulliver's Travels* (1726)

Borrow George Borrow (1803–81), writer

the Three Crofts and the Manganese companies in which Featherstone is a shareholder

Blue-Coat land pupils at charity schools, such as Christ's Hospital in London, wore distinctive blue coats

CHAPTER 33   **Mary Garth attends Featherstone. He asks her to destroy his most recent will, but she refuses. The old man dies**

From midnight, Mary Garth watches over Peter Featherstone. She smiles at the follies of the day, but is concerned that the Vincys might be disappointed in their expectation of a substantial inheritance. At three in the morning, he asks her to destroy one of the two wills he has made, which are locked in an iron chest. Mary refuses adamantly, despite his offer of money and gold. The old man cries like a child. Soon afterwards he dies.

Mary's scrupulous concern not to be seen to act dishonourably for personal gain contrasts starkly with the greed of Featherstone's predatory relatives. Her decision is not an isolated event; its repercussions shape the lives of other characters as the story unfolds.

BOOK FOUR: THREE LOVE PROBLEMS

CHAPTER 34   **Featherstone's funeral. Dorothea is alarmed to see Ladislaw in the attendant crowd**

Peter Featherstone is buried in accordance with his instructions for an elaborate funeral, conducted by Cadwallader. The rector's wife, Lady Chettam, Dorothea, and Celia, watch the occasion from an upper window in Casaubon's house. Brooke arrives. Casaubon joins the group just before Celia spots Ladislaw below. Another man, a stranger described by Mrs Cadwallader as frog-faced, is also noticed. News of

Ladislaw's arrival shocks Dorothea, who turns pale. Brooke explains that the young man is staying as his guest. Casaubon suspects that his wife has invited the young man, despite his prohibition. Brooke volunteers to fetch Ladislaw who has brought Naumann's painting.

> The physical setting, with the Chettams, Brookes, and Mrs Cadwallader looking down upon those from lower social classes reminds us of the traditional stratification of English society. The hierarchy is undergoing change with the relentless march of the middle classes, and Mrs Cadwallader voices open hostility to that process. She describes Mr Vincy as 'one of those who suck the life out of the wretched handloom weavers in Tipton and Freshitt' (p. 327).

Harpagon   a miser in Molière's play *The Miser* (1668)

omne tulit punctum   (Latin) he carried every point

Hobbes   Thomas Hobbes (1588–1679), philosopher

CHAPTER 35   **Both wills are read. Joshua Rigg inherits the estate. Fred receives nothing**

There is jealous rivalry amongst those who attend the funeral, all expectant of some share in the legacy. They assemble for the will to be read, and are disturbed by the presence of the frog-faced stranger. He is in his early thirties, and his name is Joshua Rigg. Mary Garth has seen him twice at Stone Court.

Standish, the lawyer, reads the will he drew up for Featherstone in 1825. Ten thousand pounds is bequeathed to Fred. The bulk of the remaining property and land goes to Rigg. But Standish then reads a second will, drawn up by another lawyer in 1826, with a codicil added in 1828. There is great agitation; only Rigg remains perfectly calm. He retains his legacy, and is henceforth to take the name Featherstone. The money Fred expected to receive will be used to build alms-houses for the elderly poor. Trumbull receives a gold-headed cane. The relatives bitterly bemoan their lot. Rigg coolly talks business with Standish.

Mary Garth is aware that by refusing to destroy the second will at Featherstone's command, she has blighted Fred Vincy's fortunes. Both she and he now need employment.

Middlemarch is crucially concerned with frustrated expectations. This chapter shows such expectations at their most crude and materialistic. Compared to this predatory gathering the aspirations of Dorothea and Lydgate seem all the more elevated.

The narrator who began the novel musing on St Theresa is now discussing Joshua Rigg, Featherstone's illegitimate son. There is self-conscious reflection 'on the means of elevating a low subject' (p. 341). It is recommended that the account be regarded as a **parable**. This is ironic; *Middlemarch* is a complex work of literary **realism**, not a vehicle for simple parables. George Eliot was aware that some readers might be offended by such topics, but her **epic** scope necessitated the inclusion of 'low subjects' as well as high.

batrachian frog-like

the Duke of Clarence the Duke became William IV in 1830, on the death of George IV

loobies clownish figures

Lord Grey became Whig Prime Minister in November 1830

CHAPTER 36 **Plans for Rosamond's marriage to Lydgate go ahead, despite Mr and Mrs Vincy's uneasiness about the doctor's financial prospects**

Mr Vincy admonishes Fred to return to university and pass his exams. He laments Rosamond's engagement to Lydgate, who has family connections but no money, and he vows he will oppose their marriage. Fred is faced with the prospect of having to make his own way in life. Rosamond, on the other hand, refuses to take her father's position seriously. He proves malleable to her influence, and recognises that it is too late to intervene.

Mrs Bulstrode speaks out against the match, but Vincy replies that it was her husband's trust in Lydgate which prompted his own amenability to him. Bulstrode himself laments to his wife that Lydgate has become involved with a girl who is 'obstinately worldly' (p. 347).

Lydgate receives a visit from Farebrother, who wishes to use his microscope. The doctor suggests that the stability of marriage should assist his work, although secretly he looks forward to escaping from the demands of courtship, which he considers futile.

He suggests to Rosamond that they should marry in six weeks time, arranges to take a house she likes, and buys an expensive dinner service. Rosamond, whose social aspirations are blatant, is anxious to visit Lydgate's uncle Godwin at his Quallingham estate. Lydgate is offended by Mrs Vincy's suggestion that his uncle might give the couple money, but manages to conceal his distaste.

In Christian terms, Providence refers to God's all-encompassing plan for the world. In *Middlemarch*, the word 'providence' recurs as a secular concept, indicating a naive faith that things will, of necessity, turn out well. Before the reading of the will, Fred Vincy believed in 'providence in the shape of an old gentleman's caprice' (p. 343). Now, he is faced with the need to take responsibility for his own life.

For all his progressive ideas about medical practice, Lydgate is generally conservative by temperament, and his views on gender are steeped in patriarchal assumptions. The narrator remarks that 'Lydgate relied much on the psychological difference between what for the sake of variety I will call goose and gander: especially the innate submissiveness of the goose as beautifully corresponding to the strength of the gander' (p. 356).

Santa Lucia third-century martyr, associated with cures for eye defects
Valenciennes fine lace

CHAPTER 37   **Ladislaw speaks alone with Dorothea, and the bond of sympathy between them grows. Casaubon writes to his cousin instructing him to leave the area. Ladislaw refuses to comply**

Mr Brooke has bought the *Pioneer* newspaper, in order to press the case for reform and, to Casaubon's annoyance, has engaged Ladislaw to edit it. Ladislaw feels with increasing intensity that Casaubon has wronged Dorothea by marrying her.

One day, Ladislaw is sketching at Lowick, hoping to encounter Dorothea walking. Rain drives him to seek shelter at her home. She is alone in the library, and welcomes him with 'the simple sincerity of an unhappy child visited at school' (p. 362). As they talk, he comprehends that she has married in order to assist the scholar with his work.

Ladislaw tells Dorothea about his grandmother who was disowned by Casaubon's family, and about her husband, a Polish patriot who made his living by teaching. He also speaks of his father, who died young, and of his mother who ran away from her family in order to go on stage. Casaubon financially supported Ladislaw and his mother, who died four years previously.

Ladislaw discusses the arrangement he has made with Brooke. Dorothea favours him staying but, suspecting her husband will disapprove, she suggests he should consult with Casaubon. Ladislaw departs before his cousin returns home, and Dorothea raises the matter on his behalf. Casaubon writes a letter indicating that if Ladislaw does not comply with his request to withdraw from the area he will no longer be welcome at Lowick Manor. Dorothea, meanwhile, forms a strong sense of the injustice with which Ladislaw's grandmother was treated on account of her marriage to a poor man.

The Casaubons awaken early the next morning. Dorothea suggests that her own money and property are excessive to her needs, and proposes that she offer Ladislaw assistance. Casaubon is furious. She experiences 'a dumb inward cry for help to bear this nightmare of a life in which every energy was arrested by dread' (p. 375).

The next day, a letter arrives from Ladislaw telling Casaubon that he does not share his view of the situation. He acknowledges indebtedness for past support, but denies that this enables Casaubon to curb his freedom. Casaubon receives the message in silence, but his bitterness towards Ladislaw grows.

> This is a crucial chapter for the development of a bond of sympathy between Dorothea and Ladislaw. He is aggrieved at her unsuitable marriage. She wishes to make amends for his grandmother's exclusion from Casaubon's family, on account of a marriage perceived as unsuitable. Casaubon, on the other hand, seeks to exclude Ladislaw. The young man's refusal to be dictated to intensifies Casaubon's bitterness, which later culminates in the codicil appended to his will.

> **Charles James Fox** (1749–1806), reforming politician

dark-blue freemen dark blue was the colour associated with the Liberal
party. Freemen were able to vote in parliamentary elections
Huskisson William Huskisson (1770–1830), politician, cautious reformer
killed by a train at the opening of the Manchester and Liverpool Railway
Sir Thomas Browne (1605–82), physician and author of *Religio Medici*
(1642) and other works. Widely regarded as one of the finest writers on
English prose
Delectus anthology of Greek or Latin passages for translation
Lowth probably Robert Lowth (1710–87), bishop, scholar, and poet

CHAPTER 38   **Chettam and the Cadwalladers seek to deter Brooke**
from his political activities

Chettam has lunch with the Cadwalladers. They disparage Brooke's
reformist political activities. Ladislaw's cleverness is acknowledged. He is
regarded locally with suspicion, as 'a quill-driving alien, a foreign
emissary' (p. 379). Mrs Cadwallader calls him 'a Byronic hero' and 'a
dangerous young sprig' (p. 380).

Chettam criticises the management of Brooke's estate and bemoans
the loss of Dorothea's salutary influence at Tipton Grange. Brooke's
tenants have been neglected since he dismissed the admirable Caleb
Garth, twelve years previously. Brooke drops in, only to depart unsettled,
following a concerted effort to persuade him of his folly.

Brougham and Useful Knowledge Henry Brougham (1778–1868) founded the
Society for the Diffusion of Useful Knowledge in 1825
modus money paid in lieu of a tithe
Lafitte Jacques Lafitte (1767–1844), a leader of the 1830 revolution in
France
fiat justitia, ruat (Latin) 'Let justice be done, though the world perish'

CHAPTER 39   **Chettam persuades Dorothea to advise her uncle that**
he should employ Caleb Garth as farm manager.
Brooke has a salutary encounter with one of his
tenants

Chettam summons Dorothea to Freshitt Hall to tend to Celia, who is
unwell. He voices his discontent with Brooke's situation. Dorothea then

visits her uncle and conveys excitedly Chettam's hope that Brooke will employ Garth and improve his farm management.

Ladislaw tells her that he has been banned from visiting the Casaubon home. She is 'anew smitten with hopelessness that she could influence Mr Casaubon's action' (p. 390).

Dorothea's carriage then takes her home. Her uncle accompanies her as far as a house occupied by Dagley, father of a boy who has been caught poaching. Brooke looks at the house in the light of his guilty conscience. Dagley has been drinking at market, and shows no respect for the landowner. He points out that Brooke does not fulfil in practice his promises in the radical press.

> Brooke's political ambitions end in failure. In this respect, his aspirations resemble those of Casaubon and Lydgate whose research projects are ultimately fruitless. The scholar and the doctor both neglect their wives, and are insensitive to their needs. As Chettam suggested in the preceding chapter, and as Dagley makes clear here, Brooke's negligence has caused real problems for his tenants, while he blindly pursues a grand reforming goal. In each case, obsession with general principles has precluded recognition of specific problems. Dorothea argues that 'we have no right to come forward and urge wider changes for good until we have tried to alter the evils which lie under our own hands' (p. 389).

emollit mores (Latin) it softens manners
Young Edward Young (1683–1765), poet

CHAPTER 40   **Garth receives an invitation from Chettam to manage his estate. Garth tells Farebrother that Mary refused to burn Featherstone's last will. Farebrother invites Mary to visit his mother**

The Garth family are at breakfast. Mary, who is clearly loved by the younger children, is sewing a handkerchief for Rosamond Vincy's wedding. She has been offered and has decided to accept a teaching post in York. But Chettam has invited Caleb Garth to manage his estate, and has indicated that Brooke would like him to resume work at Tipton. To general celebration, Garth instructs Mary to decline the job in York, and stay at home with her family.

In the evening, Farebrother arrives. Fred Vincy has taken the clergyman into his confidence. Garth declares that, as he now has lucrative employment, Fred's debt no longer matters. Less magnanimously, Mary says that she will think well of Fred only when he gives her good cause. Once Mary has left the room, Garth confides to Farebrother that Featherstone had requested his daughter to burn one of the wills he had made. He adds, 'if Mary had done what he wanted, Fred Vincy would have had ten thousand pounds' (p. 406). Susan Garth vigorously defends her daughter's actions.

On his way home, Farebrother encounters Mary with her little sister Letty. He invites Mary to visit his mother, who will enjoy her company. He is attracted to Mary, and considers her too fine for the crude Fred Vincy, but he suppresses his feelings.

Garth suggests to his wife that he should employ Fred Vincy to assist in managing the estate. She points out that Fred's parents would strongly disapprove. Garth reveals that Rigg and Bulstrode have both approached him to value Stone Court.

> The narrator begins this chapter with talk of 'watching effects', along the lines of a scientific experiment. This reflects George Eliot's profound interest in science, but the real issue here is point of view: 'it is often necessary to change our place and examine a particular mixture or group at some distance from the point where the movement we are interested in was set up' (p. 399). A single viewpoint is no longer adequate.

> Mary admires Farebrother, and he is clearly attracted to her. She eventually marries Fred Vincy, but an alternative does exist for her. It is one which readers might consider preferable, just as Lydgate appears a more suitable partner for Dorothea than Casaubon.

nine costly letters postal conventions of the day

Cincinnatus (c.519–438BC), Roman statesman who saved the city

CHAPTER 41   **John Raffles visits Rigg at Stone Court. Before**
              leaving, he uses a folded piece of paper to secure his
              brandy flask

Joshua Rigg is visited at Stone Court by John Raffles, his stepfather.
Raffles seeks financial assistance for Rigg's mother, but Rigg, resentful of
the maltreatment he and his mother have received from this man, knows
that Raffles will spend any money that is offered. His mother will receive
a weekly allowance, and no more.

Raffles says he will leave if Rigg gives him some brandy and a
sovereign for the journey. He uses a folded piece of paper to secure his
brandy flask within its leather case. Raffles takes the stage coach to
Brassing, where he joins the new railway.

> The folded paper is a letter from Nicholas Bulstrode. It falls by
> chance into Raffles's hands, and alerts him to Bulstrode's proposal
> to purchase Stone Court. It initiates his plan to extort money from
> the banker. Such a contrivance appears a **melodramatic** device, but
> George Eliot is illustrating the role played by accident and
> coincidence in shaping human affairs.

father-in-law stepfather

CHAPTER 42   **Casaubon, anxious about the prospects for**
              completion of his work, discusses his health with
              Lydgate. He discovers that Dorothea is aware
              that he may die suddenly

Concerned about his illness, Casaubon still hopes 'there might be twenty
years of achievement before him, which would justify the thirty years of
preparation' (p. 420). He fears that if he should die leaving Dorothea
independent possession of his property, she would fall prey to some
ruthless predator, such as Will Ladislaw.

Returning from his honeymoon, Lydgate is asked to visit Lowick
Manor. He finds Casaubon taking his habitual stroll in the Yew-Tree
Walk, and is struck by the scholar's premature aging. Casaubon speaks
of his anxiety that his work should eventually be brought to print.
Lydgate gives his diagnosis of the scholar's heart condition, and
discloses that Dorothea knows of the possibility of her husband's

sudden death. Casaubon is left 'looking into the eyes of death' (p. 424).

Dorothea joins Casaubon after Lydgate's departure, but finds her husband coldly unresponsive to her presence. He withdraws to the library, she retreats to her boudoir, feeling wretched. As she is about to send a message to her husband that she is unwell and will remain in her room, one arrives from him, indicating that he wishes to be alone that evening, and will dine in the library.

Later, suspecting that her husband has received unwelcome news from the doctor, she waits for him to come upstairs. They meet, and he speaks to her with 'kind quiet melancholy' (p. 427). Hand in hand, they walk along the broad corridor to the bedroom.

As Casaubon contemplates the prospect of imminent death, his work truncated by the failure of his own constitution, he increasingly projects his frustration and sense of failure onto the world around him. As his energies decline, he indulges in 'a perpetual suspicious conjecture that the views entertained of him were not to his advantage – a melancholy absence of passion in his efforts at achievement, and a passionate resistance to the confession that he had achieved nothing' (p. 417).

George Eliot displays considerable psychological subtlety in her portrayal of the strained marital relationship. Casaubon's egotism is such that he feels betrayed by Dorothea, who has brought the 'unappreciative world' nearer to him (p. 418). He manifests distinct paranoia in his perception of Ladislaw, whose return 'had brought Mr Casaubon's power of suspicious construction into exasperated activity' (p. 419). From this point, his actions are governed by such suspicion.

Laennec René Théophile Laennec (1781–1826), French physician whose specialism was heart disease

BOOK FIVE: THE DEAD HAND

CHAPTER 43   **Dorothea visits Lydgate's house and finds Ladislaw alone with Rosamond**

Two days later, Dorothea visits Lydgate to discuss Casaubon's health. The doctor is not at home. Dorothea seizes the opportunity to see Rosamond, but is unsettled to find her alone with Will Ladislaw. He offers to fetch Lydgate from the hospital. Dorothea insists she will go herself. Thinking of Ladislaw with Lydgate's wife, Dorothea feels confused and sheds tears. She recovers in time to converse with the doctor.

Ladislaw feels unable to continue making music with Rosamond, and says he will return another day. Rosamond later tells her husband that she believes Ladislaw adores Dorothea. Lydgate anticipates that Dorothea will give two hundred pounds annually to the new hospital.

> The music performed by Ladislaw and Rosamond contrasts with the silence prevailing at Lowick Manor. It is clear, however, that Ladislaw is besotted with Dorothea, whom he idealistically regards as a perfect woman. An element of jealousy is evident in Dorothea's reaction. So, although the couple are unable to speak to one another of their love until late in the book, readers are left in no doubt of the strong mutual attraction between them. The contrasting characteristics of Dorothea and Rosamond are shown distinctly here.
>
> **Lungi dal caro bene** (Italian) far from the well-loved
> **leather and prunella** cobblers wore leather aprons; parsons wore prunella gowns
> **Racine** Jean Racine (1639–99), French dramatist

CHAPTER 44   **After talking with Lydgate, Dorothea tells Casaubon of her plan to support the new hospital**

Lydgate tells Dorothea that her husband is displaying symptoms of anxiety. He then alerts her to the needs of the new hospital. Bulstrode's unpopularity has led to feuds which threaten the project. Dorothea grows ardent in her support. At home she tells her husband she would like to pledge an annual donation from her allowance. Casaubon distrusts his wife's motives in talking to the doctor, and suspects that she is monitoring his own precarious health.

George Eliot here uses a technique comparable to cinematic **flashback** to present events occurring during the timespan of the preceding chapter.

CHAPTER 45   **There is local opposition to the new hospital and to Lydgate**

There is opposition in Middlemarch to the new hospital and to Lydgate, who is to be its chief medical superintendent. Other medical men are unsettled by his reforming spirit; they consider him arrogant, and view his success as a threat to their livelihood.

Bulstrode has provided financial support for the hospital, but is now keen to involve other contributors, as he aims to buy Stone Court. Farebrother advises Lydgate to keep his distance from the unpopular Bulstrode, and to avoid becoming hampered by personal money matters. At home, Lydgate muses on his work while Rosamond plays the piano. Rosamond says she sometimes regrets that he is a medical man. He is intolerant of such remarks.

Mrs Dollop, in Slaughter Lane, allows us a glimpse of the lower end of the Middlemarch social spectrum. In the preceding chapter, Dorothea was easily won to Lydgate's cause when he identified his enemies as pettiness and ignorance. The figure of Mrs Dollop indicates that these enemies are not so negligible as those two idealists might assume. There is a substantial body of prejudice against Lydgate and his innovations.

Burke and Hare notorious Edinburgh murderers who sold the bodies of their victims for dissection by medical researchers

vis medicatix (Latin) healing power

St John Long (1798–1834), notorious medical charlatan

Raspail François Raspail (1794–1878), doctor and political reformer

Vesalius Andrea Vesalius (1514–64), founder of modern anatomy

Galen (c.130–200), influential Greek physician

CHAPTER 46   **Ladislaw assumes an active role in local politics. Rosamond is pregnant. Lydgate is troubled by debt**

Ladislaw has become an energetic speaker as well as a writer on political issues. He assures Brooke that popular support for Reform will soon grow. The older man lacks Ladislaw's clarity of purpose. Ladislaw's unconventional behaviour arouses local suspicion, but he is a welcome guest at the Lydgate household. Rosamond is expecting a baby. Lydgate is troubled by a bill for furniture.

> Ladislaw's character is more overtly unorthodox, but his engagement with the Reform movement aligns his ardent, passionate nature with those of Dorothea and Lydgate. The narrator admits that it is Ladislaw's 'desire to be where Dorothea was' that has brought him into the sphere of practical politics, but his commitment has subsequently grown in seriousness: 'Our sense of duty must often wait for some work which shall take the place of dilettantism and make us feel that the quality of our action is not a matter of indifference' (p. 461). The unconventional young man is regularly said to resemble a **Romantic** poet, dreaming of some lofty, unspecified goal, but by the end of the novel he has adapted to practical requirements sufficiently to become a Member of Parliament.

Lord John Russell's measure bill for electoral reform introduced in March 1831; Parliament was dissolved in April
Burke Edmund Burke (1729–97), politician and author
energumen fanatic
galligaskins breeches
Stanley Edward Stanley, Earl of Derby (1799–1869), Chief Secretary for Ireland, and later Prime Minister

CHAPTER 47   **In order to see Dorothea, Ladislaw attends a service at Lowick Church. The action proves misjudged**

Following an animated conversation with Lydgate, Ladislaw is kept awake considering his situation in Middlemarch. He assures himself that he does not aspire to marry Dorothea after Casaubon's death.

He goes the next day to Lowick Church, where he sits in curate Tucker's pew. He feels uncomfortable when Dorothea merely acknowledges him with a slight bow, and feels paralysed by the sight of Casaubon. He is pained to think that his presence might have caused discomfort to Dorothea, and returns home feeling saddened. It is now 1831.

> The narrator **personifies** Inclination and Objection in order to render dramatically the inner conflict Ladislaw experiences. *Middlemarch* is a novel which pays close attention to such psychological tensions within individuals.

Drayton Michael Drayton (1563–1631), poet
Hanover hymn tune by William Croft (1678–1727)

CHAPTER 48   **Casaubon increases his wife's involvement in his work, asking that she will complete it in the event of his death. His request troubles her. She finds him dead in the garden**

Dorothea felt that Ladislaw's presence in the church was a step towards reconciliation. She was hurt by her husband's refusal to acknowledge him. In her disappointment, 'it appeared that she was to live more and more in a virtual tomb' (p. 474).

After dinner, Casaubon and Dorothea retire to the library. He gives her a notebook containing a table of contents for his great work, and asks her to annotate it according to his instruction. Since the frank interview with Lydgate, Casaubon has sought to involve his wife increasingly in the project.

Waking in the night, Dorothea finds her husband in an armchair beside the fading fire. He asks her to continue the work they began earlier, and requests Dorothea's compliance with his wishes in the event of his death. She cannot promise to observe his instructions without knowing the details. He sleeps, but his request keeps her awake. She dreads the prospect of having to sift 'those mixed heaps of material, which were to be the doubtful illustration of principles still more doubtful' (p. 478). She is troubled by an acute awareness of her husband's labours, and recognises that she married in order to assist him.

Next morning, Tantripp, the maid, notices her paleness. As Dorothea enters the library, Casaubon is preparing to walk in the garden. He asks for an answer to his request, made the night before, and she promises to join him shortly in the Yew-Tree Walk. She feels trapped by 'the ideal and not the real yoke of marriage' (p. 481), but she then discovers her husband's dead body. Later, as Lydgate attends her, she is tormented by her failure to comply with Casaubon's request.

Casaubon's death is preceded by noticeable diminution of his energy. This decline is thrown into sharp relief by the fact that Celia has recently had a baby. Her contented and fruitful marriage contrasts with the sterility of Dorothea's 'spiritual emptiness and discontent' (p. 475). Moreover, Dorothea recognises that Casaubon's work is governed by 'a theory which was already withered in the birth like an elfin child' (p. 478).

Casaubon's work now appears to Dorothea as 'a mosaic wrought from crushed ruins' (p. 478). George Eliot is arguably registering in this description a more general loss of faith in explanatory systems of knowledge, during the later part of the nineteenth century (see Historical Background: Loss of faith).

Keble's *Christian Year* popular collection of poems, published in 1827, by John Keble

Lavoisier Antoine Lavoisier (1743–94), pioneer of modern chemistry

Gog and Magog nations led by Satan in the battle of Armageddon (Revelation 20:8)

CHAPTER 49   **Chettam is appalled by a codicil added to Casaubon's will. Speaking with Brooke, he insists that Ladislaw should be sent away from the area**

On the day following Casaubon's burial, while Dorothea is confined to her bed still in a state of shock, Chettam speaks to Brooke. Casaubon has added a codicil which Chettam recognises as 'a positive insult to Dorothea' (p. 484). Chettam insists that Ladislaw must be sent away from the area, and that Dorothea should stay with Celia and the baby. Chettam is clearly concerned that people will suppose Dorothea gave

Casaubon some reason to feel jealous of Ladislaw as a rival for her affections. Brooke, however, is keen to retain Ladislaw's services.

George Eliot patterns vocabulary carefully, in order to clarify relationships between characters. In recent chapters, both Casaubon and Dorothea have been described as 'melancholy', indicating the state of their marriage in its last stages. Similarly, the word 'disgust' was used to register the response of Chettam, Celia, and Ladislaw upon learning of the Casaubons' engagement.

George Eliot may consciously have been making a **pun** on the word 'will'. The codicil to Casaubon's will is a mean-spirited attempt to frustrate Will Ladislaw. Featherstone's will also results in frustrated hopes. But throughout *Middlemarch* the efforts of living characters to exercise their will meet with serious obstacles.

Thoth and Dagon Thoth was an Egyptian deity; Dagon was a Philistine god

Norfolk Island penal colony off the coast of Australia

CHAPTER 50   **Dorothea learns of the codicil prohibiting her marriage to Ladislaw while she remains owner of Lowick Manor. She attends to her husband's papers. Lydgate recommends the appointment of Farebrother as rector of Lowick**

Dorothea stays at Freshitt Hall, but she wishes to examine her husband's papers, and is keen to determine who should succeed him as rector of Lowick. Brooke insists there is no urgency.

After their uncle's departure, Celia reveals that Casaubon's will has decreed that Dorothea should lose Lowick Manor if she were to marry Ladislaw. Celia feels confident that her sister would never consider marrying Ladislaw, but Dorothea is in turmoil. She experiences 'a sudden strange yearning of heart towards Will Ladislaw' (p. 490).

Dorothea determines to go to Lowick in order to start to put things in order. She has the support of Lydgate, who tells Chettam: 'She wants perfect freedom, I think, more than any other prescription' (p. 491). Next day, Chettam drives her to Lowick Manor. She attends to her husband's papers, finding no intimate message, but instead a Synoptical Tabulation delineating the structure of his work.

Lydgate recommends Farebrother as a suitable successor to the living of Lowick, praising his 'plain, easy eloquence' (p. 494), while not concealing his weakness for card-playing and gambling. Dorothea longs for a display of 'primitive zeal' (p. 495), and initially favours Tyke. But she is drawn to the possibility of saving Farebrother from his weakness by materially improving his lot. Lydgate affirms that Ladislaw would also sing Farebrother's praises.

> The choice between Tyke and Farebrother to become rector recalls the earlier contest for the hospital chaplaincy. It is an opportunity for Lydgate to compensate for his earlier failure to support Farebrother, despite his friendship with him.

> Dorothea dresses as a widow. Her sombre appearance contrasts with the lavender and white dress worn by Celia. Beneath the sobriety, however, Dorothea's emotional life is revitalised by her understanding that others are capable of seeing Ladislaw as a potential suitor for her. Unlike Casaubon, who withdrew from the web of social relationships, Ladislaw is a significant, if unsettling, presence in the lives of others: 'he was a creature who entered into every one's feelings, and could take the pressure of their thought instead of urging his own with iron resistance' (p. 496).

Latimer Hugh Latimer (1485–1555), archbishop famed for his sermons
Daphnis in Greek mythology, the son of Hermes, taught by Pan to play the flute

CHAPTER 51   **Brooke's political ambitions end in chaos**

Ladislaw is not aware of the codicil, but recognises that his reputation will suffer from proximity to the recently widowed young woman. He is preoccupied with preparation for the imminent election, although Brooke has started to dissuade Ladislaw from regular attendance at Tipton Grange.

Brooke makes a chaotic electoral address from the balcony of the White Hart inn. An effigy of him appears in the crowd. His voice is mimicked and eggs are thrown. The speech draws to a premature halt. Soon afterwards, Brooke resigns his candidacy. He decides to give up the

Pioneer, and suggests that Ladislaw should find other employment. But Ladislaw is determined not to leave the area until it suits him.

Brooke refers to Ladislaw as 'a sort of Burke with a leaven of Shelley' (p. 499). These analogies may recall Dorothea's earlier perception of Casaubon as comparable to Locke and Milton. In each case allusion to representative famous men is intended to elucidate the character of their local equivalent. Distorted appraisal of Casaubon and Ladislaw results. Remember that we were initially invited to regard St Theresa as a **type** casting light on the character of Dorothea.

plumpers those who vote for only one candidate, when they might vote for more

ten-pound householders entitlement to vote was granted in the Reform Act to occupants of property valued at ten pounds or more

Pope Alexander Pope (1688–1744), poet

Johnson Samuel Johnson (1709–84), poet, lexicographer and critic

Chatham William Pitt, Earl of Chatham (1708–78), Whig statesman

Pitt William Pitt (1759–1806), second son of Chatham, twice Prime Minister

eating his dinners studying law

Althorpe John Charles Spencer, Viscount Althorpe (1782–1845), Chancellor of the Exchequer, 1830–4

CHAPTER 52   **Farebrother is appointed rector of Lowick. Fred Vincy completes his degree, and asks Farebrother to recommend him to Mary Garth**

In June, to his family's delight, Farebrother learns that he is to be rector of Lowick. A week later he receives a visit from Fred Vincy, who has completed his degree. Fred asks Farebrother to speak with Mary Garth, on his behalf, concerning the possibility of marriage if he were to become a clergyman.

Farebrother visits Mary and argues the case for Fred. She considers Fred entirely unsuited to be a clergyman, and declares 'I could not love a man who is ridiculous' (p. 516). Fred should desist from proposing until he has demonstrated his worthiness.

Farebrother mentions that he knows from her father of Mary's uneasiness concerning her refusal to burn Featherstone's second will. He assures her that the first will would not have withstood a legal challenge if the second had been burnt.

Mary senses Farebrother's love for her. Still, she declares she could never be happy knowing that Fred was unhappy on account of losing her. Her eyes fill with tears upon recognition of Farebrother's selfless generosity.

We share Mary's recognition that Farebrother loves her, and it is tempting to consider him a more appropriate husband for her than Fred Vincy. Unlike Dorothea, however, she is not blinkered by her admiration for an older man, and although she respects Farebrother, her long-standing friendship with Fred does prove a substantial basis for marriage, once he has found an appropriate direction in life.

laches legal term signifying negligence

CHAPTER 53   **Bulstrode buys Stone Court. Raffles arrives, and seeks to extort money from the banker**

Bulstrode buys Stone Court from Rigg, but does not intend to reside there until his business commitments have lessened. Rigg leaves to become a money-changer in a busy port.

One evening, Bulstrode is talking with Caleb Garth when John Raffles arrives. Raffles has been drinking, and speaks to Bulstrode with crude familiarity. He has come with news that Rigg's mother has died, but Raffles is pleased to renew acquaintance with 'Nick' Bulstrode. He alludes to the paper he used to secure his flask on his visit to Rigg as 'what you may call a providential thing' (p. 522).

Raffles refers to shameful circumstances surrounding Bulstrode's first marriage, and reveals his intention to extort money from the banker. Bulstrode gives Raffles food and drink and invites him to stay overnight. He returns to talk with him the following morning. Bulstrode is willing to pay Raffles to stay away. Raffles refuses to surrender his liberty for an annuity. Bulstrode feels 'abjectly in the power of this loud invulnerable man' (p. 529).

Raffles mentions that he had traced Sarah, the estranged daughter of Bulstrode's wealthy first wife, and had discovered the name of her husband: 'It began with L; it was almost all l's, I fancy' (p. 530). The name was, in fact, Ladislaw. That afternoon Raffles departs, leaving Bulstrode temporarily relieved, but dreading the prospect of his return.

Raffles is an incarnation of the past for Bulstrode. This is one of numerous instances in *Middlemarch* where the past's dead hand is seen to clutch the living present. Bulstrode's concern to keep Raffles at bay may recall Casaubon's efforts to remove Ladislaw from the vicinity. In both cases, the response is a defiant refusal to surrender personal liberty, although Ladislaw's sense of honour is remote from Raffles's habitually sordid conduct. Casaubon takes revenge through the codicil; Bulstrode later contrives a situation in which Raffles dies. Neither Casaubon nor Bulstrode triumphs for long, however.

Rigg's desire is to be a money-changer in a busy port. His contented materialism contrasts starkly with the insatiable idealism which drives Dorothea, Lydgate, and Ladislaw. Similarly, Bulstrode's first marriage to an old and wealthy woman reverses Dorothea's marriage to Casaubon in terms of relative ages of husband and wife and of motivation.

read himself assented to the Thirty-Nine Articles
Warren Hastings (1732–1818), agent of the East India Company, and first Governor-General of India

B OOK SIX: THE WIDOW AND THE WIFE

CHAPTER 54   **Dorothea returns to live alone at Lowick Manor. Ladislaw calls to tell her of his imminent departure for London**

Dorothea returns to Lowick Manor after three months at Freshitt Hall. Her uncle has gone abroad following the election debacle, and her friends express concern at Dorothea living alone in Lowick Manor. Mrs Cadwallader is keen that Dorothea should marry again but, aware of the codicil, she advocates intervention, fearing 'a worse business than the Casaubon business yet' (p. 538).

Dorothea feels a helpless longing to meet Ladislaw. One morning, she is attending to paperwork when he is announced. Their meeting is emotionally charged yet necessarily restrained. He intends to go to London and become a barrister, as a preliminary for public life. The arrival of Chettam hastens Ladislaw's departure.

CHAPTER 55   Prospects for a second marriage are discussed by her friends, but Dorothea vows she will not marry again

Ladislaw's departure upsets Dorothea. She is still dressed in mourning, and is not prepared to admit to herself that she has fallen in love. One warm evening at Freshitt Hall, Celia insists on removing the close cap her sister has become accustomed to wear as a widow. Mrs Cadwallader provocatively talks of errors in marriage. Later that evening, Dorothea vows to Celia that she will never marry again.

> Dorothea's characteristic inclination to self-sacrifice is to the fore in this chapter; she renounces the possibility of marrying again. Her aspiration appears typically altruistic, although it does disclose a personal need for companionship, following the loneliness of her eighteen months with Casaubon: 'I should like to take a great deal of land, and drain it, and make a little colony, where everybody should work, and all the work should be done well. I should know every one of the people and be their friend' (p. 550) (see Themes: Altruism and Egotism).

Dido queen of Carthage, deserted by Aeneas
Zenobia queen of Palmyra, enslaved by Emperor Aurelian

CHAPTER 56   The railway has come to Middlemarch. Caleb Garth and Fred Vincy protect railway agents who are physically attacked by hostile local labourers

Dorothea employs Caleb Garth to help improve her land and build cottages. She admires his efficiency, and he is impressed by her understanding of practical matters.

A railway line is to be run through Lowick parish. Local people view the innovation with suspicion and apprehension. Caleb Garth visits a farm on Dorothea's behalf. Fred Vincy, riding nearby, sees Garth and his assistant rushing to help four railway agents who are being attacked by farm labourers. Fred intervenes, winning the gratitude of Garth, whose assistant has been injured. Garth speaks to the labourers, hoping to change their perception of the new development.

Fred expresses a desire to become Garth's assistant, rather than entering the Church. He also expresses his love for Mary. Garth consults his wife before employing Fred. Susan Garth assents tearfully, after arguing that Fred is not good enough for Mary, especially with Farebrother a potential suitor.

The following morning, Garth tests Fred's writing and numeracy skills. He is dismayed at the illegibility of the young gentleman's writing, which is quite unsuitable for business, and Fred is disturbed by the prospect of desk-work. Nonetheless, Garth offers to take him on.

Fred tells his parents of the arrangement, speaking first with his father, at his warehouse. Vincy shows his displeasure, but tells Fred to stick with it now he has arrived at a decision. Mrs Vincy on the other hand is inconsolable, fearing that her son will marry Mary Garth. Vincy eventually reconciles his wife to the situation, especially as Rosamond has lost her baby, and Lydgate has money troubles. Vincy says he will not assist Lydgate, as he never really approved of the marriage.

Fred Vincy wishes to punish the labourers for their violence, but Garth recognises that its basis is pettiness and ignorance, and seeks to educate them towards acceptance of the railway. Lydgate encounters comparable resistance to his medical innovations, but instead of responding with the measured understanding shown by Garth, he chooses to ignore the opposition, and suffers the consequences. Garth, like his daughter, is a model of practical good sense. That makes his deference to his wife's view of matters all the more striking. Such considerate accommodation of another's point of view is rare in the novel, and is distant from Dorothea's experience with Casaubon, or Rosamond's with Lydgate.

CHAPTER 57   **Discussing his own prospects with Mrs Garth,
Fred Vincy learns that Farebrother is in love with
Mary**

Fred Vincy visits the Garths. Christy, their studious eldest son, is home
on holiday. Fred talks with Mrs Garth about his own prospects. She
discloses that Farebrother is in love with Mary. Fred proceeds to Lowick
Parsonage to tell Mary of Christy's arrival and of his own appointment as
her father's assistant. When Farebrother arrives, Fred feels 'horribly
jealous' (p. 578).

When they are alone, Fred tells Mary that he foresees her marriage
to Farebrother as inevitable. Mary is surprised and annoyed. She has
fleeting visions of an alternative future, but her commitment to Fred
remains unshaken.

> The presence of Christy reminds us that the Garths view education
> as an essential means of social advancement for their sons. Money
> given earlier to settle Fred Vincy's debts had been reserved to
> enable their younger son Alfred to train as an engineer. Mary, on
> the other hand, is offered no such educational opportunity. Her
> mother, for all her sympathetic kindness, is convinced that women
> should remain subordinate to men. Her ambition is that Mary
> should marry well, and Farebrother is her preference (see Themes:
> Gender).

Tully Veolan reference to Walter Scott's *Waverley* (1814)
Porson Richard Porson (1759–1808), classical scholar

CHAPTER 58   **Rosamond miscarries her baby after an accident
while horse-riding with Captain Lydgate. Her
husband's debts increase. Their furniture must be
inventoried as security against debts. Their marriage
is put under increasing strain**

Evident tensions have developed within the Lydgates' marriage. They
find a focus in Captain Lydgate, during his stay with his cousin, Lydgate.
He impresses Rosamond; her husband finds him boorish. As a
consequence of a minor accident while horse-riding with the Captain,
Rosamond gives birth prematurely to a still-born baby.

The doctor gets deeper in debt each day. Returning home one evening to find Ladislaw making music with Rosamond, he cannot conceal his ill-humour. Ladislaw tactfully departs. Lydgate tells Rosamond of his extensive debts. He has to give security, and an inventory of their furniture must be made. He insists this is a temporary measure and demands that Rosamond should not tell her father. She sobs, and suggests they move from Middlemarch to London, or closer to Lydgate's family, who live near Durham.

The couple become temporarily estranged: 'It seemed that she had no more identified herself with him than if they had been creatures of different species and opposing interests' (p. 597). A degree of accord is restored, but Lydgate anticipates with dread 'the necessity for a complete change in their way of living' (p. 598).

> Captain Lydgate features marginally in the novel, but reference to him in this chapter does highlight the radically different points of view from which Lydgate and Rosamond look at the world. The divergence in their understanding results in the increasing instability of their marriage.

> Rosamond's complete lack of respect for her husband's learning stands in stark contrast to Dorothea's initial reverence for Casaubon: 'His superior knowledge and mental force, instead of being, as he had imagined, a shrine to consult on all occasions, was simply set aside on every practical question' (p. 586). Just as Dorothea came to realise that Casaubon was not the husband for whom she had hoped, so Lydgate is no longer able to perceive his wife as a 'perfect piece of womanhood' (p. 583). Ladislaw is said to have 'more comprehension of Lydgate than Rosamond had' (p. 592). Similarly, he manifests understanding of Dorothea which her husband lacked.

the Mechanics' Institute these Institutes, established in 1820, provided education for working men

CHAPTER 59   **Ladislaw learns of Casaubon's codicil from Rosamond and is appalled**

At Lowick Parsonage, Fred Vincy hears of Casaubon's codicil. He mentions it to Rosamond, who relays the news to her husband. Lydgate instructs her not to tell Ladislaw, but she ignores him and reveals the secret. Ladislaw is appalled at his cousin's 'foul insult' (p. 601). Rosamond feels vaguely jealous of Dorothea. She is further disgruntled because, against her husband's express wishes, she has sought assistance from her father, and has been rebuffed.

> Rosamond grows increasingly defiant of her husband's instructions. She attempts to act independently, but each move creates a further tangle in the web of social relationships.

CHAPTER 60   **Ladislaw is confronted by Raffles, who knew his parents**

A few days later, Borthrop Trumbull oversees an auction of articles from a furnished mansion recently purchased by Mr Larcher, the carrier. Bulstrode has asked Ladislaw to attend in order to give his expert opinion on a picture which Mrs Bulstrode wishes to buy. After securing purchase of the picture, Ladislaw is confronted by Raffles, who asks if his mother was called Sarah Dunkirk. Ladislaw says she was, but his aggressive attitude deters Raffles from further conversation.

Later that evening, however, Raffles overtakes Ladislaw in the street and renews the conversation. This time he talks of Will's father, whom he met in Boulogne. He refers to Will's mother, running away from her own mother and the world of 'respectable thieving' in which she was raised (p. 611), to pursue a career on the stage. Ladislaw is disturbed by a sense that this unsavoury man has revealed details of her life which his mother withheld from him.

> Trumbull, with his verbal pedantry, introduces a comic element which momentarily lightens the novel's tone.

> For Ladislaw as for Bulstrode, Raffles is an embodiment of the past, giving voice to long-suppressed secrets, and altering their sense of the present. The pawnbroking business, receiving stolen

goods, which was run by Ladislaw's grandmother, discloses a tawdry facet of the march of the middle classes. Here commercial enterprise veers into criminality.

Gibbons　Grinling Gibbons (1648–1721), famous wood-carver
Guido　probably Guido Reni (1575–1642), Italian painter
'Berghems'　Nicholas Berghem (1620–83), Dutch painter
Slender　foolish young man in Shakespeare's *The Merry Wives of Windsor*
"Full many a gem", as the poet says　reference to Thomas Gray's 'Elegy Written in a Country Churchyard' (1751)

CHAPTER 61　**Raffles speaks with Mrs Bulstrode. Bulstrode recollects his involvement with the Dunkirk family, and his first marriage to Ladislaw's grandmother. He discloses that relationship to Ladislaw, and offers him compensatory payment. Ladislaw disdainfully rejects the offer**

The same night, Bulstrode returns home from business to discover that Raffles has spoken with his wife, who has only fragmentary knowledge of her husband's past, and of his first marriage. The following evening, Mrs Bulstrode notices that her husband looks unwell.

The banker muses on his past, his friendship with the Dunkirk family, and employment within their pawnbroking business. Mrs Dunkirk's husband and son died, and her daughter ran away. She grew attached to Bulstrode. Eventually they married, and he became, on her death five years after the marriage, sole inheritor of her wealth. However, he and Raffles knew that the daughter had actually been found: a circumstance which might have precluded the marriage. The inheritance would then have passed to Mrs Dunkirk's grandson, Will Ladislaw. The business collapsed after a further thirteen years, by which time Bulstrode had consolidated his position as banker, churchman, and public benefactor.

Bulstrode invites Ladislaw to meet him at his home, The Shrubs, that evening, when his wife and daughters are out. Ladislaw is struck by the banker's sickly appearance. Bulstrode discloses the ties which connect them, including his enrichment through marriage to Ladislaw's grandmother. Ladislaw feels a mixture of pity and contempt, and is disturbed by the revelation that his family has been engaged in an occupation which he considers dishonourable. His mother reacted against the stain on the family's honour, and he intends to follow her course. The repentant Bulstrode is not allowed the satisfaction of a compensatory gesture. After Ladislaw's departure he weeps 'like a woman' (p. 624), although he recovers his composure before his wife and daughters return. His sole consolation is that Ladislaw will not broadcast the evening's revelations.

> The complexity of that web of social relationships which creates the fabric of Middlemarch life is vividly rendered through the disclosure that Bulstrode married Ladislaw's maternal grand-mother, and consequently deprived him of a substantial inheritance. The revelation may recall the surprise appearance of Joshua Rigg at Featherstone's funeral, dashing Fred Vincy's hope of a legacy. In both cases we see the surfacing of connections long suppressed in the name of middle-class respectability.

> Bulstrode's particular situation is translated into a general psychological observation: 'The terror of being judged sharpens the memory: it sends an inevitable glare over the long-unvisited past which has been habitually recalled only in general phrases'. The narrator describes a man's past as 'a still quivering part of himself' (p. 615). The epic scope of *Middlemarch* enables George Eliot to encompass such insights into interior states as well as offering a coherent portrait of English provincial life in the early 1830s.

CHAPTER 62   **Dorothea is upset by Mrs Cadwallader's adverse remarks concerning Ladislaw and Rosamond. She returns home to find Ladislaw waiting for her. He announces his imminent departure from Middlemarch**

Next morning, Ladislaw determines to leave Middlemarch as soon as possible. He writes to Dorothea asking to see her once more before his departure.

Dorothea is visiting her sister at Freshitt Hall. At Chettam's contrivance, Mrs Cadwallader broaches the subject of Dorothea's relationship with Ladislaw. She comments on the impropriety of his regular visits to Rosamond's house. Dorothea protests at this misrepresentation of his behaviour. Mrs Cadwallader laments Lydgate's unsuitable marriage. Dorothea departs haughtily before anything further can be said. On the drive to Tipton Grange she weeps.

Returning home, Dorothea finds Ladislaw in the library. He speaks of the insult he has suffered through Casaubon's will. She assures him that she never doubted his integrity. Their feelings cannot be expressed openly, and neither is sure how the other really feels. Dorothea initially suspects that he loves Rosamond, with whom he has spent more time alone, but after his departure she is filled with the sense that Ladislaw does love her.

Driving to Lowick Manor she overtakes Ladislaw walking, and he raises his hat. He remains unsure whether she loves him. After spending the evening with the Lydgates, he departs the following day.

Mrs Cadwallader's lamentation over Lydgate's unsuitable marriage corresponds to her reaction to Dorothea's marriage, and forms a small link between the experiences of those two characters.

An unspoken love has developed between Dorothea and Ladislaw. While it remains unspoken, and subject to interpretation, there is ample room for each to doubt the nature of the other's feelings.

'weepers' black crape veils worn by widows

BOOK SEVEN: TWO TEMPTATIONS

CHAPTER 63   **Farebrother learns of Lydgate's financial problems**

At a Christmas dinner party, Farebrother discusses Lydgate's work for the new hospital and is told that Lydgate has financial problems. There is speculation that he may receive support from his wealthy relatives.

At a New Year's Day party hosted by Vincy, Farebrother tells the doctor that he will lend a friendly ear when needed. Lydgate, who has helped advance Farebrother's situation, is nonetheless mortified by the offer of help. He feels his private life has been exposed to public view.

Mary Garth's popularity with Mrs Vincy's youngest daughters softens their mother's view of her. Farebrother's relatives still hope he may marry Mary.

The contrast between altruism and egotism is a major theme of *Middlemarch*. Some characters (such as Bulstrode) are governed in their actions by self-interest. Others (such as Dorothea) are driven by desire to assist others. Farebrother is an altruistic man, but helping others depends upon their receptivity, and Lydgate's self-esteem bridles at Farebrother's supporting voice (see Themes: Altruism and Egotism).

a Ken and a Tillotson famous seventeenth-century clergymen and writers

CHAPTER 64   **As his debts deepen, Lydgate decides to lease his house. Rosamond takes steps to ensure this does not happen, and writes to Lydgate's uncle, asking for money**

Lydgate requires a thousand pounds to clear his debts. His mood deteriorates and his relationship with Rosamond grows increasingly troubled as circumstances become more straitened. He suggests that they find cheaper accommodation, and says that Ned Plymdale (Rosamond's former suitor), who is to marry Sophy Toller, might be interested in their house and furniture. Rosamond is reduced to tears, and filled with resentment. In silence she leaves the room, resolved to hinder her husband's plans. She visits Ned Plymdale's mother, then Trumbull's office, where she countermands her husband's instruction to lease their property.

That evening, she tells Lydgate that she has visited Ned Plymdale's mother and has ascertained that he has found another house. He discloses the extent of his debts. The next day she writes to Lydgate's uncle, Sir Godwin, asking for money. On New Year's Day no reply has arrived, but Rosamond confesses that she has cancelled her husband's instructions to Trumbull. Lydgate is thrown into inner turmoil as his wife chastises him for not attaining the social position she had anticipated when they married. Lydgate, unaware of his wife's letter, considers with distaste the prospect of a visit to his uncle seeking financial assistance.

This sequence of events preceded the party at which Farebrother sought to console Lydgate. This is an example of the technique, comparable to cinematic **flashback**, which George Eliot uses to supply another angle on events.

In the preceding chapter we saw the strength of Lydgate's self-esteem. Is it inexcusable pride, or an acceptable concern for personal honour? In this chapter, Rosamond's self-esteem drives her to contradict her husband's instructions. There is vanity in her response, but that failing is surely made worse by Lydgate's habit of treating her as a child. Their marriage resulted from selfish concerns: Lydgate saw Rosamond as a decorative enhancement; she saw him as a means to social elevation. In effect, they now inhabit separate worlds.

George Eliot shows that Rosamond's dependent femininity, which is largely a product of her education, prevents her attaining sympathetic understanding of Lydgate's precarious position (see Themes: Gender). The doctor shows no understanding of the reasons underlying 'her negative character — her want of sensibility, which showed itself in disregard both of his specific wishes and of his general aims' (p. 652). Rosamond, on the other hand, cannot comprehend that 'the Lydgate she had been in love with had been a group of airy conditions for her, most of which had disappeared' (p. 661). Mary Garth's compassionate and practical response to Fred Vincy's money troubles provides an obvious contrast.

CHAPTER 65 **A condescending letter arrives from Lydgate's uncle**

Lydgate intends to visit his uncle at Quallingham, but keeps the plan from Rosamond. Then, a letter arrives from Sir Godwin. Rosamond excitedly presents the letter to her husband. He is furious. The letter is contemptuous of a man who gets his wife to beg on his behalf. Sir Godwin declares he cannot make any useful connections for his nephew, asserting 'I have nothing to do with men of your profession' (p. 664).

Rosamond cries at Lydgate's angry words. He criticises her secrecy and deviousness. She confronts him with failure to provide for her in an appropriate fashion, says he has exposed her to ridicule, and proclaims dramatically: 'I wish I had died with the baby' (p. 667). He embraces her as she weeps, but he is unable to say anything.

> Many of the social relationships in *Middlemarch* are presented in terms of the exercise of power by one individual over another. For example, Featherstone derives obvious pleasure from the control he wields over Fred Vincy and Mary Garth. Lydgate shows a glimmer of sympathetic understanding when he recognises that Rosamond has no such distraction from wretchedness as his own work provides for him. But the limits to his understanding are telling: 'it was inevitable that in that excusing mood he should think of her as if she were an animal of another feebler species. Nevertheless she had mastered him' (p. 667). The concluding sentence casts the patriarchal figure as the loser in a struggle. He seems incapable of conceiving marriage as a state of mutual respect.

CHAPTER 66 **Lydgate plays billiards in a desperate attempt to win money. Farebrother exhorts Fred Vincy to act in a manner deserving of Mary Garth's love**

Lydgate grows increasingly desperate. One evening, he visits the Green Dragon inn hoping to purchase a cheaper horse from Bambridge. He plays billiards and starts to win money. Fred Vincy arrives, and is astonished to find his brother-in-law behaving so uncharacteristically. Farebrother arrives just as the doctor has started to lose money. Lydgate greets him politely, then leaves. The rector asks Fred to accompany him to St Botolph's church. Farebrother speaks of his own affection for Mary, and exhorts Fred to conduct himself in a manner worthy of her affection.

> The narrator has earlier referred to character as 'a process and an unfolding' (p. 149). Lydgate's uncharacteristic behaviour is a good illustration of the way circumstances may determine the nature of that process and unfolding (see Characterisation).

chapter 67   **Bulstrode is taken ill, and Lydgate advises him to rest. The doctor alludes to his own money troubles, but Bulstrode offers no help**

Next morning, Lydgate feels ashamed that he has added to his debt. He now views Rosamond's suggestion that they should leave Middlemarch as a distasteful possibility. Despondently, he considers approaching Bulstrode for assistance. He has noted a deterioration in Bulstrode's health, and commensurate loss of his energy invested in the hospital.

He is called to attend to Bulstrode at the bank. Lydgate diagnoses stress, and advocates that the banker refrain from business for a while. Bulstrode declares his intention to spend time by the coast. He will withdraw support from the hospital.

Lydgate discloses his own financial difficulties. Bulstrode, who feels he has given enough support to his brother-in-law's family, suggests unsympathetically that the doctor should declare himself bankrupt.

In seeking help from Bulstrode, Lydgate is again acting in an uncharacteristic manner. His hopes are dashed not because Bulstrode feels animosity towards him, but because the banker perceives him in the context of Vincy's family. This is further evidence that however much individual characters may aspire to live independently, they are inextricably caught up in a web of social relationships.

chapter 68   **Raffles continues his extortion of money from Bulstrode. Bulstrode invites Caleb Garth to manage Stone Court**

This chapter takes us back to Christmas Eve. Raffles reappears at The Shrubs. Bulstrode considers it prudent to keep him there, rather than sending him into town. But the drunken Raffles proves 'hopelessly unmanageable' (p. 686). Bulstrode grows defiant, and early on Christmas Day he escorts the unwelcome guest from his premises, giving him one hundred pounds with promise of more if he stays away.

Bulstrode asks Caleb Garth to manage Stone Court. Garth advises him to let the property and take part of the proceeds annually. Bulstrode accedes to a proposal that Fred Vincy should manage the farm under Garth's supervision.

As the various strands of the novel develop, chronological disruptions in the storyline and leaps back in time become increasingly necessary to supply information we need in order to make sense of events.

Bulstrode likes to be in control, and to manipulate others. He gives money to Raffles believing it will hasten his self-destruction through drinking and dissolute living. In this belief he is proved correct, but before long it becomes apparent that control of an individual is not enough to ensure control of events, which have unforeseen ramifications.

CHAPTER 69   **Garth encounters Raffles, who is unwell, and takes him to Stone Court. He informs Bulstrode who summons Lydgate to assist. Garth says he no longer feels able to work for the banker. Bulstrode offers to settle the doctor's debts**

On the day Bulstrode refuses assistance to Lydgate, Garth visits the banker's office. He has encountered Raffles on the road, clearly very ill, and has taken him to Stone Court. Bulstrode sends for Lydgate. Garth declares himself unable to work for Bulstrode any more as Raffles has told him of the banker's past. Garth later informs his wife that he has detached himself from association with Bulstrode.

The banker rides to Stone Court, anxious to arrive before Lydgate. Despite the disagreeable nature of their earlier conversation, the doctor complies with Bulstrode's request to attend the sick man. He diagnoses a serious but not fatal condition, and advocates constant monitoring and total abstinence from alcohol. Bulstrode decides he should look after the patient personally.

While returning to his home, Lydgate considers with dread the prospect before him. Arriving, he finds the inventory is being taken. Rosamond has taken to her bed. She is persuaded not to return to her parents, but the marriage is immensely strained.

Bulstrode takes comfort from the fact that his secret has been exposed to Garth and not some less discreet person. Earlier, he felt justifiably confident that Ladislaw would not disclose any details of his past. But he recognises the need to limit the damage Raffles may cause, and under the guise of offering altruistic assistance towards a sick man, and to the financially troubled doctor, he endeavours to protect his self-interest (see Themes: Altruism and Egotism).

Dr Ware John Ware (1795–1864), American physician, and author of a treatise on alcoholism

CHAPTER 70   **Raffles dies. Lydgate is uneasy at the circumstances surrounding the death, but relieved that his financial problems have been resolved**

Bulstrode examines the contents of Raffles's pockets to trace his previous whereabouts. Then he sits with the sleeping man. Next morning, Lydgate leaves opium to be administered in small doses if Raffles becomes sleepless. Bulstrode writes a cheque to cover the doctor's debts. That evening he entrusts Raffles to the care of Mrs Abel, his housekeeper, but deliberately omits to specify the limit of the dosage. He also gives her the key to his wine-cooler where brandy is kept. Next morning, Lydgate arrives in time to witness the death of Raffles. He feels uneasy about the circumstances, but says nothing.

At home, Lydgate is visited by Farebrother, who has grown concerned about the doctor's uncharacteristic behaviour. He is astonished to find Lydgate cheerful. The doctor tells the rector that Bulstrode has advanced him money to pay his bills. Privately, he is unsettled by his awareness that Bulstrode's change of heart was followed so swiftly by the death in his house, but he talks of his plans to economise and ensure a brighter future.

Farebrother, concerned at Lydgate's uncharacteristic behaviour, now finds him cheerful. It is again apparent that character is not simply a fixed entity, but is shaped by circumstances, and is inaccurately assessed if considered in isolation from changing contexts. Farebrother takes the lesson on board; in Chapter 72 he observes that 'character is not cut in marble – it is not something solid and unalterable. It is something living and changing, and may become diseased as our bodies do' (pp. 734–5) (see Characterisation).

Who should be considered responsible for Raffles's death? Lydgate, who supplied the opium? Mrs Abel, who administered the fatal dose in combination with alcohol? Bulstrode, who withheld vital information? Or Raffles himself, who destroyed his own health through excessive drinking? An event, like a character, is never entirely self-contained. Interpretation of this death may vary according to one's point of view.

the Political Unions beginning in 1830, these societies were formed to agitate for reform

CHAPTER 71   **Bambridge, the horse dealer, has heard from Raffles the story of Bulstrode's disreputable past. He spreads the news. Bulstrode is forced to resign from public positions. Dorothea determines to restore Lydgate's reputation, which has been tarnished by association**

Outside the Green Dragon, Bambridge tells friends that at Bilkley horse fair he heard Raffles's account of how Bulstrode had acquired his wealth. Hopkins, the draper, exclaims that he has recently furnished Raffles's funeral at Bulstrode's expense. Others gather round to hear the story elaborated.

Hawley speaks of the matter with Farebrother, sparking in his mind an unwelcome association between Lydgate's relief from debt and his service to Bulstrode in attending Raffles. Connections are made less sympathetically by others, and gossip concerning the banker's alliance with the doctor spreads through Middlemarch.

A meeting is convened to discuss the town's response to a case of cholera. Bulstrode and Lydgate happen to arrive together. There is a call for Bulstrode's resignation from public positions, on account of the allegations levelled by Raffles. Lydgate helps the suddenly frail banker leave the room, while feeling bitterness at perceived guilt by association. After the meeting, Brooke, accompanied by Farebrother, drives to see Dorothea. Both are concerned about the position in which Lydgate has been placed. Dorothea insists that they should actively seek to clear Lydgate's name.

Despite Bulstrode's precautions, gossip spreads, forming a web which traps him, and also ensnares Lydgate. Speculation is woven around the basic facts and produces various interpretations, but predominantly these denigrate the reputations of both men. The dead hand of the past grips the present, as it did through the wills of Featherstone and Casaubon.

Dorothea's faith in Lydgate confirms the fundamental affinity between them. While maintaining her high ideals, she is increasingly committed to practical action as a means to help others.

Botany Bay penal colony in Australia

went over to the Romans the Duke of Wellington (1769–1852) changed his view and became a supporter of Catholic emancipation

Act of Parliament passed in 1828, making provision for improved sanitation

BOOK EIGHT: SUNSET AND SUNRISE

CHAPTER 72   Dorothea urges action on behalf of Lydgate

Dorothea is dissatisfied with Farebrother's 'cautious weighing of consequences' in relation to Lydgate. She would prefer 'ardent faith in efforts of justice and mercy' (p. 733). Over dinner with the rector and the Chettams, she asks 'What do we live for, if it is not to make life less difficult to each other?' (pp. 733–4). Chettam insists that the doctor must act for himself. Dorothea, discouraged by the company, bursts into tears.

> Dorothea's **rhetorical question**, 'What do we live for, if it is not to make life less difficult to each other?', shows that her idealism has survived her unfortunate marriage. It has always been combined with practical altruism, in her plans to build cottages, and now, on a more personal basis, in her determination to restore Lydgate's reputation as an honourable man.

CHAPTER 73   Lydgate considers likely consequences of the loss of Bulstrode's reputation

After taking Bulstrode home, Lydgate rides several miles out of Middlemarch to think matters over. He deduces the truth of Bulstrode's situation, while preserving room for charitable doubt. He also comprehends how he is now viewed by the people of Middlemarch. He resolves to defend his honour and to stand by Bulstrode, but he feels weighed down with anticipation of Rosamond's reaction.

> The narrator offers a sympathetic view of Lydgate's plight: 'Only those who know the supremacy of the intellectual life – the life which has a seed of ennobling thought and purpose within it – can understand the grief of one who falls from that serene activity into the absorbing soul-wasting struggle with worldly annoyances' (p. 737). Practical characters, such as Caleb Garth and his daughter, appear in a positive light in *Middlemarch*. They are well equipped to deal resourcefully with life's daily challenges. Those who aspire to loftier achievements are frustrated and damaged by such 'annoyances'.

> The Garths keep the world on an even keel, but the idealists aspire to improve it. Invariably, such idealism is eventually compromised. Dorothea will become a wife and mother. Lydgate will give up research and become a successful practitioner. Still, in George Eliot's view, each spark of idealism moves the world forward a little.

CHAPTER 74   **Mrs Bulstrode learns of her husband's disgrace. She adopts simple dress, and pledges her loyalty to him**

Rosamond and her aunt, Mrs Bulstrode, are implicated in local gossip. Mrs Bulstrode has felt unsettled about her husband since he brought Raffles home, and she asks Lydgate whether anything untoward has happened. He gives nothing away, so she goes to town in search of news. Eventually, her brother spells out the misfortune that has befallen her. People will talk, whatever the truth may be, and he wishes they had never heard of Bulstrode or Lydgate.

Back home, she retires to her room, entrusting care of her husband to her daughters. She changes her clothes, dressing now with plain simplicity. When she rejoins her husband, his anguish is palpable, and she feels compassionate and tender towards him. They shed tears together: 'His confession was silent, and her promise of faithfulness was silent' (p. 750).

Mrs Bulstrode's faithfulness to her husband appears admirable, especially when compared with the way her niece has responded to problems in her marriage with Lydgate. But when she adopts simple dress as an act of humility, we may recall the demands of loyalty made upon Dorothea by Casaubon. In that light, the supporting role allocated to wives may appear repressive, and Mrs Bulstrode's self-sacrificing compliance may appear less worthy of unquestioning respect.

Newgate famous London prison

CHAPTER 75   **Rosamond's spirits are lifted by clearance of Lydgate's debts and news of Ladislaw's imminent arrival. Then, she hears of the scandal surrounding Bulstrode and her husband. She is devastated**

Once immediate financial threat has been lifted, Lydgate seeks to mend his marriage. Rosamond feels unfulfilled, and is keen to move to London. She misses Will Ladislaw, whom she takes to be an admirer. A letter arrives from Ladislaw, indicating an impending visit to Middlemarch. This, and removal of the debt, lifts her spirits. She arranges a dinner party for friends, without telling Lydgate. The invitations are declined. Lydgate is furious when he finds out what has happened.

Feeling hurt, Rosamond visits her parents. The Vincys disclose the scandal of Bulstrode and its implications for Lydgate. Rosamond is now adamant that they must move to London.

Rosamond's response to her husband's troubles contrasts dramatically with that of her aunt in the previous chapter. It is tempting to see Mrs Bulstrode in a positive light, and to cast Rosamond in negative terms. But Mrs Bulstrode's upbringing results in obedient compliance, while Rosamond's education has led her to expect social advancement as a reward for her feminine charm. Her disobedience, like her aunt's loyalty, results from a well-defined view of the social role of women. The extremes they seem to represent may be closer together than is immediately apparent.

CHAPTER 76   Dorothea offers support to Lydgate

A few days later, Lydgate is summoned to Lowick Manor. Dorothea wishes to support the hospital. She is struck by the change in his looks. Lydgate reveals he may be leaving Middlemarch. She praises his integrity, and asks him to explain the circumstances which led to harmful gossip. He welcomes an opportunity to speak with a benevolent friend, and tells his side of the story.

Dorothea offers to support his work, in the hope that one day his reputation will transcend the damage done by scandal. He speaks of his obligations to his wife, who now fervently wishes to leave the area. Dorothea volunteers to speak with her, affirming her own desire to assist his 'power to do great things' (p. 767). She writes a cheque for one thousand pounds, enabling Lydgate to clear his debt to Bulstrode.

> The narrative has affirmed an underlying affinity between Dorothea and Lydgate; both are idealists who wish to help others, especially the less fortunate, and both become trapped in unfortunate marriages. As a woman, Dorothea does not feel able to aspire to greatness through her own actions but she continues to hope that she can help a man 'do great things'. She speaks with a 'child-like grave-eyed earnestness' (p. 765), indicative of her acceptance of the superior capabilities of men. Lydgate will not achieve greatness, but George Eliot believed that even unsuccessful striving produces small changes towards gradual social improvement.

CHAPTER 77   Dorothea finds Ladislaw alone with Rosamond

Next day, Lydgate goes to a nearby town called Brassing. Rosamond remains at home, melancholy, yet eagerly awaiting the arrival of Ladislaw.

Dorothea also has Ladislaw on her mind. His reputation locally has suffered from the disclosures concerning Bulstrode. Arriving at Lydgate's house, hoping to speak with Rosamond, she finds Ladislaw clasping the hands of the doctor's tearful wife. He is evidently moved at the sight of Dorothea, but she hurriedly explains she is delivering a letter for Lydgate, and retreats from the room. Overcoming her emotional turmoil, she visits Chettam and her uncle, intent upon clearing Lydgate's name.

In the preceding chapter, Dorothea pledged ardent support for Lydgate's work. Here, she is thrown into turmoil when she finds Ladislaw with the doctor's wife. The strength of her jealousy is a measure of the love she feels for Ladislaw, an emotional attachment of a different order to her respectful feelings for Lydgate.

CHAPTER 78   **Rosamond, feeling rejected by Ladislaw, displays greater warmth towards her husband**

After Dorothea's hasty departure, the atmosphere between Ladislaw and Rosamond is tense. He responds furiously to her sarcastic suggestion that he should pursue Dorothea and make plain his preference for her. Ladislaw has lost the consoling certainty that Dorothea believes in him, but his devotion to her is total: 'No other woman exists by the side of her' (p. 778). Rosamond is devastated to discover that far from being held high in his esteem, she is excluded from Ladislaw's deeper feelings. Suddenly, 'her little world was in ruins' (p. 780). The word 'little' reminds us of the constraints placed upon Rosamond's comprehension of events. It shows her incapacity to transcend the narrow limitations of her understanding, while suggesting that her perception is blinkered on account of her upbringing as a young woman of the provincial middle class.

Lydgate returns home to find his wife lying on her bed in a state of distress. He comforts her, and senses an unaccustomed warmth in her response. He erroneously assumes this is the beneficial effect of Dorothea speaking on his behalf.

Ladislaw speaks to Rosamond with brutal frankness. This is a measure of his frustrated passion for Dorothea. It also has a salutary effect, as it breaks down the barrier of her egotism: 'What another nature felt in opposition to her own was being burnt and bitten into her consciousness' (p. 779). A degree of sympathy with others has been admitted, and this is manifested in her increased warmth towards Lydgate (see Themes: Altruism and Egotism).

CHAPTER 79   **Lydgate talks with Ladislaw about the damage caused by their connections with Bulstrode**

Lydgate finds the letter left by Dorothea. Then Ladislaw arrives, and the doctor tells him that Rosamond is unwell. Lydgate speaks of the scandal which has degraded his own and Ladislaw's reputation within Middlemarch. He notes a change in Ladislaw's demeanour when Dorothea is mentioned, and suspects that she is the real reason for his presence in the locality. He projects a future in which their friendship will be renewed in London.

> Ladislaw has rejected Bulstrode's offer of financial assistance and believes he has cut himself free. Lydgate, on the other hand, accepted the banker's money. The crucial difference lay in their circumstances, rather than in strength of character. Indeed, there is an underlying affinity between them; both aspire to improve the world around them, and both are intolerant of pettiness and ignorance. They are also comparable in their anxiety concerning the future prospects for their high aspirations: 'We are on a perilous margin when we begin to look passively at our future selves, and see our own figures led with dull consent into insipid misdoing and shabby achievement. Poor Lydgate was inwardly groaning on that margin, and Will was arriving at it' (p. 783).

CHAPTER 80   **Dorothea continues to defend Lydgate, and grows increasingly aware of her love for Ladislaw**

Dorothea dines with Farebrother and his family, and takes the opportunity to explain that Lydgate has been a victim of circumstance. Mention of Ladislaw flusters her, and she leaves hastily. At home, alone, she is overcome with grief and moans tearfully, 'Oh, I did love him!' (p. 786).

Next day she forces herself to relive the previous day's experiences. She feels that she has been unjust to Rosamond, whom she was intending to enlighten and support. Looking from her window, she sees the early morning stirrings of working people, and intuits 'the largeness of the world and the manifold wakings of men to labour and endurance' (p. 788).

She instructs Tantripp to bring her new dress, and lays aside her more sombre mourning garments. She has resolved to live actively, and the fresh garments are an outward aid to that resolve. She then walks towards Middlemarch, intent on helping Rosamond Lydgate.

Dorothea feels helpless in her love for Ladislaw, and cries like a child. But that suggestion of immature dependency contrasts with the mature capacity for sympathy she then demonstrates. 'Was she alone in the scene? Was it her event only?' (p. 787) she asks, forcing herself to pass beyond her own subjectivity and see matters from the points of view of the other participants. Looking from her window she sees people starting work, and the range of her sympathies is extended still further: 'She was a part of that involuntary, palpitating life, and could neither look out on it from her luxurious shelter as a mere spectator, nor hide her eyes in selfish complaining' (p. 788).

mummy pulpy substance

White of Selborne Gilbert White (1720–93), curate and author of *The Natural History of Selborne* (1788–9)

CHAPTER 81   **Dorothea speaks with Rosamond of Lydgate's integrity, and is told of Ladislaw's love for her**

Lydgate is preparing to leave as Dorothea arrives at his house. He gives her a letter, offering thanks for her generous assistance. He leaves the women to talk.

Rosamond is anxious, but Dorothea clasps her hand with 'gentle motherliness' (p. 793), and speaks with 'self-forgetful ardour' (p. 795) in defence of Lydgate's character and behaviour. Rosamond sobs. Dorothea speaks of the peculiar obligations which marriage brings. They embrace, then Rosamond declares that Dorothea is mistaken in her interpretation of the previous day's events. She reveals that Ladislaw declared his total commitment to love for Dorothea.

Lydgate returns, and Dorothea leaves the couple to rebuild their relationship.

Speaking with Lydgate, Dorothea appeared 'child-like'. When counselling Rosamond her 'motherliness' surfaces. Her decision to act, rather than remain passive, has brought her maturity. She is 'self-forgetful' when she defends Lydgate. That capacity to transcend egotism is a lesson which Rosamond needs to learn, and the embrace between the women suggests that learning process has begun (see Themes: Altruism and Egotism).

CHAPTER 82   **Ladislaw learns that his love for Dorothea is reciprocated**

After a day away from Middlemarch, Ladislaw returns to spend a discomforting evening with the Lydgates. He returns to his hotel room and reluctantly reads a note passed to him by Rosamond. It indicates that all has been explained to Dorothea, who consequently holds him once again in high esteem.

Rosamond's note is a 'self-forgetful' gesture, showing that she has learnt sympathy from Dorothea. Her discretion, in committing the message to paper rather than blurting it out, shows a mature understanding lacking from her earlier actions.

the Rubicon   stream in Italy. In 48BC, Julius Caesar crossed it with his army. This was taken as a declaration of war. 'To cross the Rubicon' consequently means to take an irrevocable step

CHAPTER 83   **Ladislaw visits Dorothea at Lowick Manor. They declare their love for one another**

Miss Noble arrives at Lowick Manor, a go-between from Ladislaw, who wishes to see Dorothea. Soon, Ladislaw appears in the library. He proclaims his devotion to Dorothea and kisses her hand. She is visibly moved.

Outside there is a storm. The couple smile at one another, and talk with an underlying sense that their love is hopeless. They hold hands 'like two children' (p. 810). They kiss, then move apart. Ladislaw is furious with frustration that they can never be married. When he says goodbye, Dorothea cries out that she hates her wealth, and says that if he leaves her heart will break. He holds her in his arms, and she affirms that they can live well on her own inheritance.

The breaking of the storm can be seen as **symbolic** of the lovers' suppressed passion rising to the surface. The couple are compared to children, suggesting their feeling of helplessness. This is overcome because Dorothea is decisive. She insists that her future will be with Ladislaw, and that she will surrender Lowick Manor. The adjective 'queenly' is applied to her in these concluding chapters, indicating that she has taken control of events, for the moment at least.

CHAPTER 84   **Dorothea's family and friends are distressed at her engagement to Ladislaw, but she refuses to change her mind**

Mr Cadwallader walks with Chettam on the lawn at Freshitt Hall. Mrs Cadwallader talks with Celia and Chettam's mother. Brooke arrives. It is assumed that his evident dejection has been caused by the failure of the Reform Bill, but he reveals that its source is actually Dorothea's decision to marry Ladislaw in three weeks time. The news is received with disbelief.

Celia goes to Lowick to try to exert sisterly influence. Dorothea is delighted to see her, but rejects her advice. Celia points out that they will not be able to meet after the marriage, on account of Chettam's disapproval. Dorothea plans to move to London with Ladislaw.

> **The Not-Browne Mayde** late fifteenth-century song
> **the Lords had thrown out the Reform Bill** in May 1832; however, it was passed in June 1832
> **Draco and Jeffreys** Draco, who lived in the seventh century BC, and Judge Jeffreys (1648–89) were notorious for their judicial severity

CHAPTER 85   **Bulstrode prepares to leave Middlemarch. His wife asks him to help Vincy's family. He asks her to persuade Garth to resume supervision of Stone Court**

Bulstrode prepares to leave Middlemarch, haunted by the sense that he is not the man he has pretended to be. He dreads that his wife might come to perceive him as a murderer. Their daughters have been sent away to boarding school to shield them from the crisis. Mrs Bulstrode asks her husband to assist her brother's family. He points out that Lydgate, Vincy's son-in-law, is unlikely to accept help, as he returned the previous loan. Mrs Bulstrode recognises the moral rejection implied by that settled debt, and weeps.

Bulstrode suggests that Fred might be helped if Garth could be persuaded to assume management of Stone Court. He indicates that persuasion must come from his wife.

Bulstrode's habitual selfishness has been broken down. At last, he manifests concern for the well-being of others (see Themes: Altruism and Egotism).

CHAPTER 86   **Caleb Garth tells Mary that Fred can become manager of Stone Court. Mary breaks the news to Fred**

Mary is in the garden when Caleb Garth arrives home. They discuss her love for Fred. He then announces that Fred may live at Stone Court, overseeing it for his aunt Bulstrode. This would enable the young couple to marry. Fred arrives, and Garth leaves Mary to convey the news to him.

It is appropriate that the honest and practical Garth family occupies the concluding chapter. They are a touchstone for decency and integrity, even though lofty thoughts are alien to them.

FINALE

Fred and Mary's marriage results in 'a solid mutual happiness' (p. 832). Fred achieves distinction as a farmer. Mary publishes a book of stories, written initially for her three sons.

Lydgate dies at fifty, after establishing an excellent practice and writing a treatise on gout. He provides handsomely for his wife and four children. Rosamond subsequently marries a wealthy, elderly physician.

Dorothea never regrets giving up her fortune to marry Will Ladislaw. She remains actively philanthropic, while being both wife and mother. Ladislaw becomes a reforming Member of Parliament. Brooke keeps in correspondence with the rebellious couple, and an invitation to visit Tipton Grange, coinciding with news that Dorothea has given birth to a son, helps heal the family rift. Brooke lives long, then leaves his estate to Dorothea's son.

Chettam always deplores the marriage to Ladislaw, a view shared by Middlemarch public opinion which disparages both of Dorothea's marriages. But the children of Dorothea Ladislaw and Celia Chettam grow up to be good friends.

> The narrator surveys the course followed by the lives delineated in the preceding narrative. There is no room for close scrutiny of their subsequent experiences, so a potted history must suffice. Literary **realism** satisfies readers' desire for knowledge. The overview fortifies the illusion that these characters have existed beyond the pages of a book.

> George Eliot affirms through her narrator that gradual social improvement is not brought about solely by the great. Unacknowledged contributions are made by those who act with genuine sympathy and compassion for others. Dorothea's influence is difficult to calculate, 'for the growing good of the world is partly dependent on unhistoric acts, and that things are not so ill with you and me as they might have been, is half owing to the number who lived faithfully to a hidden life, and rest in unvisited tombs' (p. 838).

basil plant alludes to John Keats's poem 'Isabella' (1820)
Municipal Reform the English Municipal Corporations Reform Act (1835)
Cyrus Cyrus the Great, founder of the Persian Empire

PART THREE

CRITICAL APPROACHES

CHARACTERISATION

One of the basic assumptions of literary realism is that readers should feel they know the characters in a novel. Description of physical appearance plays its part; for example, we are told that Farebrother is 'a handsome, broad-chested but otherwise small man, about forty, whose black was threadbare: the brilliancy was all in his quick grey eyes' (pp. 161–2). But there must be psychological coherence as well: behaviour should be explicable, and motives should be credible. George Eliot assists our understanding by contrasting different temperaments, as in the dialogues between Dorothea and Celia. Parallels also assist characterisation; an underlying affinity sheds light on both Dorothea and Lydgate.

Characterisation of individual figures is sustained with remarkable consistency throughout this long novel. The author's achievement is all the more striking as *Middlemarch* repeatedly asserts that character is not merely a fixed entity; it develops in response to circumstances, and may change according to context. The narrator affirms that character 'is a process and an unfolding' (p. 149). Farebrother observes that 'character is not cut in marble – it is not something solid and unalterable. It is something living and changing, and may become diseased as our bodies do' (pp. 734–5).

Linked to this point is another which complicates the rendering of character. George Eliot insists that an individual character should not be viewed in isolation, but as part of a web of social relationships. The point is distilled in the assertion that 'there is no creature whose inward being is so strong that it is not greatly determined by what lies outside it' (p. 838).

In addition, characters are subject to speculation or gossip, which offers an alternative interpretation of character and behaviour. This interpretation may be mistaken, yet still have significant impact on events. Dorothea's initial view of Casaubon prompts the narrator to remark: 'Signs are small measurable things, but interpretations are illimitable, and in girls of sweet, ardent nature, every sign is apt to conjure up wonder, hope, belief, vast as a sky, and coloured by a diffused thimbleful of matter in the shape of knowledge' (p. 25). Lydgate, on the other hand, experiences difficulties, as an outsider in Middlemarch, partly because he is 'known merely as a cluster of signs for his neighbours' false suppositions' (p. 142).

Despite these complications, individual characters are drawn with sufficient clarity to enable summary:

ARTHUR BROOKE

Brooke, a country squire and magistrate around sixty years old, has never married, but is guardian to his nieces, Dorothea and Celia. His kindliness is combined with a rambling mind, reflected in his speech. His benevolent intentions are increasingly seen to be outweighed by problems arising from his self-absorption. Cadwallader describes him as 'a very good fellow, but pulpy; he will run into any mould, but he won't keep shape' (p. 70). This pulpiness is evident in his failure to alert Dorothea adequately to potential problems in her marriage to Casaubon. It is also evident in his political campaigning, which entirely lacks substance. He talks vaguely of reform, while the living conditions of his own tenants deteriorate as a result of his stinginess.

DOROTHEA BROOKE

A young woman of unusual beauty, Dorothea dresses with Puritanic plainness to indicate that she is free from personal vanity. Yet there is a kind of pride in her aspiration to be more than a feminine adornment, and to help shape the world. Her sister Celia calls her Dodo, with obvious affection, but Dorothea's ardent seriousness often unsettles those who meet her. Celia regards her with 'a mixture of criticism and awe' (p. 15).

Dorothea's idealism seems out of place in provincial England where, in the early 1830s, the materialistic values of the commercial middle-class were becoming increasingly influential. She wishes to channel her religious passion into plans for social improvement. She has started an infant school in the village, and her cherished project is to build cottages for local labourers. As a woman, however, there are clear limits to what she can achieve in this patriarchal society, and she becomes dependent upon the capacity of men to act.

In her marriage to Casaubon an inclination to self-sacrifice is marked; she is filled with 'hopeful dreams, admiring trust, and passionate self-devotion' (p. 71). Such subordination seems inescapable for an intelligent woman in a society designed to promote masculine values. She is heiress to Tipton Grange only in the sense that her son inherits it on her uncle's demise. She has no personal entitlement.

Her friends compare her intelligence unfavourably with her sister's common sense. Dorothea's cleverness does not prevent her making serious errors of judgement, notably in her willingness to marry Casaubon. She consistently looks beyond the requirements of day-to-day living. Celia remarks, 'You always see what nobody else sees; it is impossible to satisfy you; yet you never she what is quite plain. That's your way Dodo' (p. 36). Her intensity produces practical problems, but George Eliot suggests that such vision, often at personal expense, is necessary for the gradual improvement of human society.

At the end of *Middlemarch*, Dorothea marries Will Ladislaw and becomes a wife and mother, although she is still actively philanthropic. Feminist critics have seen this move into contented domesticity as unacceptable capitulation to patriarchal demands. But the compromise shows her acknowledging her own emotional needs as a human being. Her determination to act for herself, very evident at the end of the novel, is an important step away from childlike dependency towards self-fulfilment, in the face of society's disapproval.

CELIA BROOKE

Affectionately called Kitty by her elder sister Dorothea, Celia is amiable and sensible. Those qualities win approval generally withheld from Dorothea's lofty aspirations. She makes the marriage which her sister declined, and lives happily with Sir James Chettam and their children. Her contentment is attained within clear limits, however, and while social reform is the big topic of the day, she settles for the stability of a conservative life.

EDWARD CASAUBON

The scholarly Casaubon inhabits a world of knowledge from which Dorothea, as a woman, has been excluded, and to which she craves entry. This is the basis for their marriage. Her narrow education, described as a 'toy-box history of the world' (p. 86), combines with her ardent imagination to envisage this world as a place of wonders. She is totally devoted to her husband's grand project, seeking to uncover the key to all mythologies. Casaubon has moments of despondency, 'toiling in the morass of authorship without seeming nearer to the goal' (p. 85). But it is Casaubon's cousin, Will Ladislaw, who discloses to Dorothea that the scholar's ignorance of German has left him unaware of work which renders his own obsolete.

Casaubon, who has lived in Lowick Manor for ten years, is a fairly wealthy man, around forty-five years old. He looks older, with iron-grey hair, deep eye-sockets, spare form and pale complexion. His eyesight is beginning to fade. Dorothea, in her blinkered idealism, compares him to the philosophers Locke and Pascal, and the poet Milton. Others see him more clearly. Chettam calls him 'a dried bookworm' (p. 22). Mrs Cadwallader calls him 'a great bladder for dried peas to rattle in' (p. 58), and jokes that when a drop of his blood was placed under a microscope 'it was all semi-colons and parentheses' (p. 71). Brooke thinks he is destined to be a bishop, but Casaubon dies of a heart-attack, after a life of futile labour and unreflecting egotism.

SIR JAMES CHETTAM

Chettam is a handsome baronet, a 'blooming Englishman of the red-whiskered type' (p. 16). He is described as amiable and he knows the limits of his abilities, so he and Celia Brooke are obviously compatible. Initially, he hopes to marry Dorothea, but being a man who cares little for ideas he does not meet her demands. He does implement her plan for cottages on his estate, however, even after the marriage to Casaubon. This may indicate his continuing admiration for her; certainly, he shows concern for her and is outraged at both her marriages. But Chettam seems genuinely altruistic; he is highly critical of Brooke's lapses in caring for his tenants. A less charitable interpretation might suggest that, in a period of agitation for reform, it is politically advantageous for a member of the aristocracy to preclude discontent amongst his own tenants.

Eᴸɪɴᴏʀ ᴄᴀᴅᴡᴀʟʟᴀᴅᴇʀ

The wife of the rector of Tipton and Freshitt is 'a lady of immeasurably high birth' (p. 53), a member of the De Bracy family. She belongs to the old aristocracy, but is happily married to a man from a lower social class. Nonetheless, she is an inveterate snob. Her pedigree gives her confidence to speak in a forthright manner, and she injects a note of caustic humour into her comments on Middlemarch life.

Hᴜᴍᴘʜʀᴇʏ ᴄᴀᴅᴡᴀʟʟᴀᴅᴇʀ

The rector of Tipton and Freshitt is 'a large man, with full lips and a sweet smile; very plain and rough in his exterior, but with that solid imperturbable ease and good-humour which is infectious' (p. 68). He is a tolerant man, free from egotism and contented with an unassuming rural existence. For a clergyman he shows remarkably little interest in theology, but is devoted to fishing.

Wɪʟʟ ʟᴀᴅɪꜱʟᴀᴡ

The grandson of Casaubon's aunt Julia, Ladislaw has inherited her grey eyes, quite close together. He has light brown curls, and a 'delicate irregular nose with a little ripple in it' (p. 79). He was educated at Rugby School and the University of Heidelberg, but has not settled to a career. Rather, he travels across Europe, studying art, and other manifestations of the poetic imagination.

The contrast to his scholarly cousin could not be more dramatic. Ladislaw is compared to the dashing **Romantic** poets Shelley and Byron. He writes poetry, sings, and draws pictures. He declares that his religion is 'to love what is good and beautiful when I see it' (p. 392). He has a lively sense of humour, is fond of children, and befriends Farebrother's eccentric aunt, Miss Noble. He aims to conduct himself with honour and integrity, but his passionate and spontaneously rebellious nature at times results in unruly behaviour and inconsiderate outbursts.

He becomes Dorothea's second husband, and is elected as a reforming Member of Parliament, yet since the novel's publication there have been critics who have protested that Ladislaw is too lightweight to bear the significance allocated to him. They have detected a lack of adequate **realism** in George Eliot's portrayal of a figure who 'looked like an incarnation of the spring whose spirit filled the air – a bright creature, abundant in uncertain promises' (p. 471). It has been suggested that he serves primarily to heighten our sense of Dorothea's real worth, after the folly of her marriage to Casaubon.

TERTIUS LYDGATE

Lydgate has 'heavy eyebrows, dark eyes, a straight nose, thick dark hair, large solid white hands' (p. 114). There is 'a certain careless refinement about his toilette and utterance' (p. 92). His voice is 'deep and sonorous' (p. 125). After studying medicine in London, Edinburgh, and Paris he arrives in Middlemarch, aged twenty-seven, and assumes responsibility for supervision of the new hospital. He introduces new medical practices, and is passionately concerned for reform of his profession, and for innovative research.

His idealism and 'intellectual passion' (p. 144) disclose an affinity with Dorothea. Like her, he is reputedly 'very clever' (p. 91), and he is keen to help others, especially the poor. He has chosen a profession that requires 'the highest intellectual strain' while keeping him 'in good warm contact with his neighbours' (p. 165).

He regards science as 'the inward light which is the last refinement of Energy, capable of bathing even the ethereal atoms in its ideally illuminated space' (pp. 164–5). But his quest for a primitive tissue from which all others are derived is destined, like Casaubon's search for the key to mythologies, to end in failure.

The name Tertius indicates that he is a third son, and so is disadvantaged in terms of inheritance, even though he is well-connected, being related to the aristocratic Lydgates of Northumberland. He is determined to make his own way in the world, and enters his profession with zeal, but money troubles increasingly compromise his lofty aspirations. He is contemptuous of pettiness and ignorance, but his arrogance prevents him addressing them directly, in order to overcome them.

During his time in Paris he was passionately infatuated with an actress who killed her husband. This was an uncharacteristic lapse of self-control for a man whom Fred Vincy calls a prig. Lydgate's father was a military man, although, like Dorothea, he was orphaned early. On his own request, his guardians apprenticed him to a country medical practitioner.

His marriage to Rosamond is as debilitating as Dorothea's marriage to Casaubon. They inhabit separate worlds of understanding and have no interests in common. He sees his wife through a lens of deeply ingrained patriarchal assumptions. He 'was no radical in relation to anything but medical reform and the prosecution of discovery. In the rest of practical life he walked by hereditary habit' (pp. 348–9). After leaving Middlemarch he becomes a successful practitioner in London before dying at fifty.

Mr BULSTRODE

Nicholas Bulstrode the banker is an outsider, 'altogether of dimly known origin' (p. 96), who married Mr Vincy's sister. His speech is fluent and subdued. He is around sixty years old, has 'pale blond skin, thin grey-besprinkled brown hair, light-grey eyes and a large forehead' (p. 123). A respected professional man and philanthropist, pious in religion, he is eventually exposed as a hypocrite and ruthless opportunist, who serves only his self-interest.

He has considerable social power, stemming largely from his control of personal loans and charitable allocations. But he acted unscrupulously in the past and concealment has become 'the habit of his life' (p. 824). The past returns to haunt him in the figure of John Raffles, who extorts money from him. He fears he will become 'an object of scorn and an opprobrium of the religion with which he had diligently associated himself' (p. 615). He is eventually driven by disgrace to leave Middlemarch.

Mr and mrs vincy

Walter Vincy, mayor of Middlemarch, is a florid and fleshy man, who has made money from his manufacturing business. He is a respectable figure, but spends his days at the warehouse, and belongs to a different social class to the inhabitants of Tipton Grange and Freshitt Hall. He has 'expensive Middlemarch habits', spending money on coursing, his cellar, and dinner parties (p. 230). His sister, Harriet, is married to Nicholas Bulstrode.

His wife Lucy, forty-five years old, radiates good humour. She was an innkeeper's daughter, and has a 'tinge of unpretentious, inoffensive vulgarity' (p. 158). She appears snobbish, however, when suggestion arises that Mary Garth may marry her son Fred. Mrs Vincy's sister was the second wife of the wealthy Peter Featherstone.

Rosamond vincy

The beauty of Mr Vincy's daughter Rosamond, a graceful, blue-eyed blonde, is widely admired by the men of Middlemarch. In consequence, 'every nerve and muscle in Rosamond was adjusted to the consciousness that she was being looked at. She was by nature an actress of parts that entered into her *physique*: she even acted her own character, and so well, that she did not know it to be precisely her own' (p. 117). Her education has trained her to be ladylike, with an emphasis on feminine elegance, and an avoidance of weighty matters. She is a fluent pianist. Lydgate is attracted to her as a decorative adornment, but she is strong-willed, and her obsession with social rank and material advancement places their marriage under considerable strain.

It is tempting to see Rosamond as a shallow egotist, but Lydgate's sense that 'in poor Rosamond's mind there was not room enough for luxuries to look small in' (p. 701) is unfair. Rosamond is 'clever with that sort of cleverness which catches every tone except the humorous' (p. 159). She is too self-conscious to make jokes, and that self-consciousness is the product of her narrow education and of her upbringing by well-meaning but socially ambitious parents.

Dorothea is dazzled by the prospect of a hidden world of knowledge. Rosamond is beguiled by the lifestyle of the upper classes, which lies beyond the social horizon of her middle-class manufacturing family. Lydgate attracts her because he comes from beyond that horizon, and evokes 'vistas of that middle-class heaven, rank' (p. 118). Her mother's disparaging remarks about the Garth family indicate that Rosamond has been trained to aspire to 'that celestial condition on earth in which she would have nothing to do with vulgar people' (p. 166). She is undoubtedly selfish, but it is not simply a personal failing.

FRED VINCY

Rosamond's brother Fred is good-natured, but is recognised as 'the family laggard' (p. 97). He is evidently unsuited for business. Fred's idleness is in part due to his expectation that he will receive a substantial legacy from Peter Featherstone. That expectation is disappointed. Mr Vincy wishes him to train for the clergy, and Fred eventually completes his degree. However, he lacks the vocation, and is pleased to be apprenticed to Caleb Garth as a farm manager. He eventually becomes a successful farmer. His love for Mary Garth remains unwavering through the financially troubled phase of his life, and is rewarded with a happy marriage to her.

PETER FEATHERSTONE

Featherstone is a wealthy old invalid, whose second wife was Mrs Vincy's sister. Fred Vincy regularly visits him at Stone Court, anticipating a substantial legacy, as the old man is thought to be childless. But it transpires that Featherstone has an illegitimate son, Joshua Rigg, who inherits the estate.

The old man derives sadistic pleasure from humiliating Fred. He also enjoys being cruel to Mary Garth, whom he employs to look after him: 'It was usual with him to season his pleasure in showing favour to one person by being especially disagreeable to another, and Mary was always at hand to furnish the condiment' (p. 133). He stops her reading while she sits with him. In his confrontationally patriarchal view 'Home Sweet Home' is 'the suitable garnish for girls' (p. 116).

MARY GARTH

Mary is small and broad-featured, with brown curly hair. Her plainness is accentuated when she is in the company of Rosamond Vincy, who regards her as 'sensible and useful' (p. 113). Unlike Rosamond she has a pronounced sense of **ironic** humour. She tends to talk in generalities rather than speaking of particular cases, drawing broad lessons from specific experiences, rather than indulging in gossip. She is a character who sees things plain, largely due to her remarkable capacity for detachment, and she reports what she sees with frank honesty. She has no ambition to change the world, but her practicality and sympathetic nature create the conditions for friendly social relationships and a happy marriage.

MR AND MRS GARTH

Caleb Garth, Mary's father, is a kindly surveyor, valuer, and land-agent. He is a man of great integrity and honesty, who refuses to participate in any activity which might be considered disreputable. His practical knowledge is widely recognised, and he is sought after as a farm manager. He reveres work and has a passion for machinery, but he pays little heed to money, and at the start of the novel he is still reeling from the failure of his building business. He is a rounded man, who wants his son Alfred to become an engineer, but also loves music. Importantly, he respects his wife, and invariably consults with her before arriving at any significant decision.

Susan Garth was a teacher before she married Caleb. She is 'the same curly haired square-faced type as Mary, but handsomer, with more delicacy of feature, a pale skin, a solid matronly figure, and a remarkable firmness of glance' (p. 244). She has four sons and two daughters. She is generous and intelligent, but adheres to the belief that women should subordinate their interests to those of men.

CAMDEN FAREBROTHER

Farebrother is 'a handsome, broad-chested but otherwise small man, about forty, whose black was very threadbare: the brilliancy was all in his quick grey eyes' (pp. 161–2). He is an affable and outgoing clergyman, whose passion is the study of Natural History. This interest helps him establish a sympathetic relationship with Lydgate. His preaching is 'ingenious and pithy' (p. 178), delivered without a book, and it draws a good congregation. He lives with his mother, sister, and aunt. Farebrother is in love with Mary Garth, but stands aside to enable Fred Vincy to marry her.

JOSHUA RIGG

Rigg is Featherstone's illegitimate son, now in his early thirties. He has bulging eyes, a 'thin-lipped, downward-curved mouth, and hair sleekly brushed away from a forehead that sank suddenly above the ridge of the eyebrows' (p. 332). He is 'sleek, neat, and cool' like the frog he resembles (p. 413), and has 'a high chirping voice' (p. 340). He has worked as a clerk and accountant in a small commercial business in a seaport. After selling Stone Court to Bulstrode, he achieves his materialistic ambition of becoming a money-changer in a busy port.

JOHN RAFFLES

Approaching sixty, Rigg's stepfather John Raffles is 'very florid and hairy, with much grey in his bushy whiskers and thick curly hair'. He is stout and has 'the air of a swaggerer' (p. 413). He has spent ten years in America supported by money from Bulstrode. He now seeks to extort more money, threatening to expose the banker's sordid past. He becomes very ill due to alcoholic poisoning, and dies at Stone Court, while in Bulstrode's care.

THEMES

ALTRUISM AND EGOTISM

Characterisation in *Middlemarch* is conceived between the poles of altruism and egotism. Characters change, but each may be measured at any point in the story against a scale that ranges from selfless concern for the well-being of others, to obsessive self-interest. George Eliot undoubtedly expected her readers to consider altruistic behaviour preferable to self-centredness.

The flaws of the novel's evident egotists (such as Casaubon, Bulstrode, and Rosamond Vincy) are clear enough. The narrator remarks: 'Will not a tiny speck very close to our vision blot out the glory of the world, and leave only a margin by which we see the blot? I know no speck so troublesome as self.' (p. 419). But the altruists also have their failings. Dorothea initially appears haughty and naive in her idealistic outlook. Lydgate's determination to advance the medical profession makes him lamentably inconsiderate at home. Caleb Garth helps others without demanding payment, but as a result his business collapses and his family faces financial difficulty.

The problem is that what is good for one person may have harmful effects upon others. This is compounded by the distortions which, as the narrator observes, enter into one person's interpretation of another's wishes: 'But how little we know what would make paradise for our neighbours! We judge from our own desires, and our neighbours themselves are not always open enough even to throw out a hint of theirs' (p. 520).

In the short-term acts of selfish egotism exert powerful influence upon the course of events. Nonetheless, George Eliot recognised that practical acts of altruism, such as Dorothea's plans to build cottages, Lydgate's concern to improve the medical profession, and Ladislaw's career as a reforming politician, all contribute in some small way to the gradual improvement of human society.

THE WEB OF SOCIAL RELATIONSHIPS

There are a number of characters in *Middlemarch* who aspire to control the course of their own lives. They are invariably frustrated in their aspiration. A major theme of the novel is that social relationships form a web which produces interdependence among the characters. No action takes place in isolation; consequences are often unforeseen.

The web provides a structural principle for relationships between various parts of the story. In thematic terms it emphasises limits upon the capacity of individuals to determine their own destiny. As the lives of individuals are inextricably bound to the actions and attitudes of others, a capacity for sympathy is vital. This does not merely involve feeling sorry for others, but necessitates an ability to conceive how life might appear from another's point of view. Throughout *Middlemarch*, Dorothea struggles to achieve such sympathetic understanding.

At the end of the book, she has become Mrs Ladislaw, a wife and mother, performing small philanthropic acts. George Eliot seems to suggest that this circumscribed role, falling so far short of Dorothea's earlier ambitions, is the best she can hope for. In a modern democratic society it is not individual heroism, but reforming Acts of Parliament and technological change, such as the advent of the railway, which shape the world in obvious ways. The impact of personal kindness is far less visible, although in the long term it may prove equally important.

In this novel, the individual appears diminished in importance, and that has unsettled some readers, but George Eliot believed that small acts of personal generosity play their part in a gradual evolution towards social improvement. So, in the web of social relationships, each human being should be seen as 'the slow creation of long interchanging influences' (p. 409).

THE GENERAL AND THE PARTICULAR

One of the most noticeable characteristics of the narrator is a persistent tendency to draw general conclusions from specific cases. We may regard this an aspect of narratorial omniscience, although the voice has less in common with an all-knowing God than with a scientist deriving laws from particular observations. The narrator's practice seems to be summed up in Lydgate's remark that the 'mind must be continually expanding and shrinking between the whole human horizon and the horizon of an object-glass' (p. 640).

The novelist Henry James (1843–1916) felt that George Eliot actually worked in the other direction, moving from the abstract to the concrete, and after her death he wrote critically in the *Atlantic Monthly* that her characters and situations evolved from the concerns of her moral consciousness, rather than from direct observation of life. It may be that in a world where religious and scientific certainties no longer offered consolation and assurance, George Eliot was searching to establish tenable moral principles through such generalisation. It has the effect of drawing readers into the frame; we are made to recognise that an apparently localised event may have relevance for us, in our lives.

But to counter Henry James's criticism, we might note the narrator's observation that, 'There is no general doctrine which is not capable of eating out our morality if unchecked by the deep-seated habit of direct fellow-feeling with individual fellow-men' (p. 619). Sympathetic understanding rather than abstract moral principle is the real requirement. It is an evident failing that Dorothea's 'ardent nature turned all her small allowance of knowledge into principles, fusing her actions in their mould' (p. 193). The important change she undergoes in the course of the book is away from this tendency, towards a commitment to act practically in response to the particular needs of other people. The narrator affirms the necessity for such practical action, for 'even while we are talking and meditating about the earth's orbit and the solar system, what we feel and adjust our movements to is the stable earth and the changing day' (p. 525).

SOCIAL CLASS

The historical dimension of *Middlemarch*, set forty years before its actual composition, draws attention to processes of social change. In English society such change has invariably led to changes in the relationship between social classes. The title of the novel may be a conscious pun, suggesting the march of the middle class. George Eliot portrays English society across the class spectrum, from the baronet Sir James Chettam, through members of the gentry such as Brooke and Casaubon, the successful, commercial middle class, such as Bulstrode and the Vincys, the lower middle class Garth family, and working class characters such as Dagley. But it is a society in transition, and the kind of influence which accrues, for better or worse, to a man such as Bulstrode is an indication of a changing structure of social power. Does the narrator reveal an affinity with any particular class?

GENDER

The relationship between men and women is clearly an important theme in *Middlemarch*. The novel portrays a patriarchal society, that is, one in which conventionally masculine values are dominant. That dominance had been challenged by writers such as Mary Wollstonecraft, in her *Vindication of the Rights of Woman* (1792) and, more recently, by John Stuart Mill in *Subjection of Women* (1869). George Eliot was cautious in her view of the need for change in gender relationships. She always favoured gradual evolution over militant clamour. But Dorothea and Rosamond clearly suffer on account of the limits imposed on their view of the world by their upbringing and their education.

Patriarchal assumptions are evident in Chettam's conviction that masculinity is in itself an advantage. Men are superior to women, he believes, 'as the smallest birch-tree is of a higher kind than the most soaring palm' (p. 21). Arthur Brooke's condescending view of Dorothea's aspirations is manifested in a series of patronising remarks, such as, 'We must not have you getting too learned for a woman, you know' (p. 338), and 'deep studies, classics, mathematics, that kind of thing, are too taxing for a woman' (p. 65).

In an essay called 'Silly Novels by Lady Novelists', written for the *Westminster Review* in 1856, George Eliot criticised lightweight fiction written by women, because it tended to fuel prejudice against 'the more solid education of women'. Lack of solid education proves a damaging obstacle in Dorothea's and Rosamond's relationships with their husbands. Lydgate wants his wife to be docile. He distrusts clever women, such as Dorothea: 'It is troublesome to talk to such women. They are always wanting reasons, yet they are too ignorant to understand the merits of any question, and usually fall back on their moral sense to settle things after their own taste' (p. 93).

For much of the nineteenth century, daughters received little formal education, unless their parents had sufficient wealth to pay for special tutelage. Even then, the quality of the experience was markedly lower than for their male counterparts. Social accomplishments such as playing the piano, 'a small kind of tinkling which symbolized the aesthetic part of the young ladies' education' (p. 45), were considered a more fitting training than intellectually challenging subjects. George Eliot felt that women should have equal access to basic knowledge. She refused to be dogmatic, however; education should meet different needs.

Fred Vincy goes through the motions of taking his degree at university, but his temperament befits him for practical work. Mary

Garth, who has been bullied by Peter Featherstone, and prevented from reading in his company, eventually writes a book. But she was raised by a mother who viewed the subordination of women to men as proper, and significantly Mary's book is not a feminist tract but relates stories of great men.

Some of George Eliot's close friends, such as Barbara Bodichon, sought reforms in the spheres of law, politics, and education. George Eliot harboured suspicions that such reforms would impair women's capacity for compassionate action. She felt that women have a capacity for empathy which is often missing from patriarchal conduct, and wished to promote this quality, but remained unsure how best that might be done.

GEORGE ELIOT'S LITERARY REALISM

George Eliot's early work displays her commitment to a fairly straightforward conception of **realism**, in which the writer's obligation is to produce an accurate representation of the known world, a faithful reflection of people and the way they live.

By the time she wrote *Middlemarch*, matters had become more complex. She still aspired to represent the known world, but she recognised that knowledge itself had become fraught with problems. This was especially the case since she had lost the certainties of youthful religious zeal, and she saw that many other intellectuals had similarly lost faith in orthodox Christianity.

In *Middlemarch*, shared understanding has evidently been displaced by conflicting interpretations. Casaubon's work has been superseded by new theories offered by German scholars. Lydgate finds himself at odds with older doctors over his innovative methods and attitudes. On a more mundane level, local labourers view the railway as a dangerous presence in their locality, while Caleb Garth seeks to assure them of its benefits. Perhaps Henry James had this fragmentation of understanding in mind when he wrote, in *Galaxy* magazine in 1873, that *Middlemarch* sets a limit to 'the development of the old-fashioned English novel'. Simple realism, based on a common sense of knowing the world, no longer seemed viable.

A customary requirement of literary **realism** is that neither language nor style should obtrude. A priority of this kind of writing is to enable readers to feel that they know the characters and communities depicted. If language and style lose their transparency they distract attention from the story and complicate our sense of understanding. George Eliot introduces humour into her novel with the character Borthrop Trumbull, 'an amateur of superior phrases' (p. 310), who relishes words for their own sake and consequently appears rather foolish.

Middlemarch is primarily a realist novel, but it is concerned with the complexities of psychological states, and was written with a late nineteenth-century awareness that knowledge, in science and philosophy, had become provisional and unstable. So although language is approached foremost as a vehicle for the story, George Eliot also directs us to the fact that words are used in differing ways in different contexts. This suggests that no single way of speaking about the world is adequate to understand it completely.

The **epigraphs** which head each chapter reflect the changing nature of the English language, from Geoffrey Chaucer (*c.*1340–1400) through to George Eliot's own invented quotations. There are also quotes in Spanish, French and Italian. We may recall that it is Casaubon's ignorance of German that blinds him to the limitations of his own work.

George Eliot also includes **dialect**, representing the manner of speaking particular to the Middlemarch area. Fred Vincy says to Rosamond that 'All choice of words is slang. It marks a class' (p. 99). Local dialect in *Middlemarch* marks the working class characters, such as Dagley in Chapter 39, or the labourers in Chapter 56. It is indicative of the characters' limited horizons. Their usage is steeped in a traditional way of living, without the education which has steered members of the middle classes towards a standardised way of speaking English. In Chapter 24, Mrs Garth endeavours to teach her youngest children 'to speak and write correctly, so that you can be understood', unlike old Job, the labourer whose quaint way of speaking seems to belong to an earlier age (p. 244).

Fred criticises poets who persist in archaic usages inappropriate to their time, calling an ox 'a *leg-plaiter*' (p. 99). That antiquated term referred to the way oxen walked, crossing their legs with each step. It is picturesque, but old-fashioned. George Eliot's vocabulary, on the other hand, is appropriate to life in an England where the railway had arrived and industrial towns and cities thrived.

She introduces words from contemporary science, conveying a sense of the age, and bolstering characterisation of the doctor, Lydgate, and of Farebrother who has a passion for natural history. Such words also indicate that a specialised vocabulary contributes to a different model of understanding. Medical knowledge leads to a perception of human beings which is very different to that held by theologists, philosophers, painters, or poets.

METAPHORS

In Chapter 10, the narrator observes that 'we all of us, grave or light, get our thoughts entangled in metaphors, and act fatally on the strength of them' (p. 85). The remark is intended to cast light upon Casaubon's flawed conception of the ways of the world. It refers to a **metaphor** drawn specifically from economics: the scholar's expectation of 'a compound interest of enjoyment' stored up during his years as a bachelor (p. 85). In a novel where Bulstrode, a banker, exercises considerable social influence, and where Lydgate and Fred Vincy are troubled by debts, the metaphor has particular resonance. George Eliot uses metaphors to trace such threads running through this long novel. They allow us to make telling connections.

Images of mirrors and windows are used metaphorically in *Middlemarch* to signal problems arising with regard to knowledge of the self and of its relationship to the world. For example, Lady Chettam reports that her son, James, considers Dorothea to be 'the mirror of all women' (p. 91). Here, the mirror suggests not an accurate reflection but an idealised picture of her. Dorothea's sense of confinement within a sterile marriage is conveyed by the view from the bow-window, which frames 'the still white enclosure which made her visible world' (p. 274). The image of the pier glass which opens Book Three is a more extended and elaborate metaphor addressing the way in which one's sense of self shapes one's perception of the world.

As the narrator's observation indicates, we use metaphors as an aid to understanding, but they tend to entangle our thoughts and mislead us. Another prominent metaphor that recurs in the book is the labyrinth, suggesting the maze of confused and conflicting impressions and expectations that form a large part of human experience. Characters such as Casaubon and Lydgate, professionally engaged with issues of knowledge, hope to find a thread to lead them through the labyrinth, but none materialises.

Another prominent metaphor, the web, illustrates that threads followed by individual characters only lead to entanglement with the lives of others. Nobody lives in isolation; a social web binds together the fortunes of disparate persons.

NARRATIVE TECHNIQUE

STRUCTURE

Middlemarch is divided into eight books, each of which bears a title that hints at the principal concern of that phase of the story. The books are framed by a brief prelude and finale.

George Eliot began with the intention of writing two stories, one entitled 'Miss Brooke', the other depicting life in the provincial town of Middlemarch, with a young doctor as the main character. These separate stories were subsequently fused in the first eighteen chapters of the novel. Out of this fusion the novelist developed an elaborate series of parallels in terms of character, event and theme, enabling her to bind the various strands of this massive book into close relationships. So, Dorothea's passionate nature is mirrored in Lydgate's intensity; both make unsuitable marriages; and both eventually compromise their idealism.

As already discussed, one of the presiding metaphors of *Middlemarch* is the web. The plot of the novel itself resembles a web. As it unfolds relationships are disclosed connecting apparently discrete characters. Will Ladislaw discovers that his grandmother was formerly married to Bulstrode. There are many other less obvious links, and chains of events with unforeseen consequences. George Eliot recognised that this network of social relationships placed limits upon the capacity of individuals to shape the course of their own lives. This had significant implications for her characterisation of figures such as Dorothea,

Lydgate, Casaubon, and Ladislaw, all of whom strive for personal goals which are denied to them by circumstances beyond their control.

These parallels and connections have impressed critics with a sense of the novel's structural integrity. Despite the size of the book, George Eliot leaves no loose ends. She manages to bring together an overview of an historical period and a place, with accounts of the intimate experiences of individual characters, rendered through a series of dramatic scenes. These scenes often involve tense encounters, with characters confronting one another in states of heightened emotion. Often, the scenes involve mistaken interpretations of actions or intentions, which later result in further scenes of similar intensity.

EPIGRAPHS

Each chapter is headed by an **epigraph**, a brief quotation which focuses attention upon a major issue addressed in that chapter. Many of these quotations are derived from earlier literature, and their sources are acknowledged. Unacknowledged quotations were invented by George Eliot herself, but serve the same purpose.

NARRATIVE VOICE

The narrative voice is a prominent element in *Middlemarch*, steering us through the account of events and shedding light on characters' motives and reactions. It would be naive to regard this voice as a straightforward vehicle for George Eliot's personal views. The author is creating it as a device to complicate and enrich our responses. It can be both critical and sympathetic, and can vary in tone. Is it the voice of a woman or a man? To what social class does she or he belong?

Middlemarch follows the example of Henry Fielding (1707–54) in its use of an **omniscient narrator**, but for George Eliot this omniscience was compromised by the same scepticism which precluded her belief in an all-knowing God. A significant number of her contemporaries shared this scepticism. The narrative voice in *Middlemarch* is omniscient in the sense that it has access to characters' thoughts, and can report separate events occurring simultaneously, but it always implies the possibility of other points of view.

PART FOUR

TEXTUAL ANALYSIS

TEXT 1   (PAGES 264–5)

> Let the high Muse chant loves Olympian:
> We are but mortals, and must sing of man.

An eminent philosopher among my friends, who can dignify even your ugly furniture by lifting it into the serene light of science, has shown me this pregnant little fact. Your pier-glass or extensive surface of polished steel made to be rubbed by a housemaid, will be minutely and multitudinously scratched in all directions; but place now against it a lighted candle as a centre of illumination, and lo! the scratches will seem to arrange themselves in a fine series of concentric circles round that little sun. It is demonstrable that the scratches are going everywhere impartially, and it is only your candle which produces the flattering illusion of concentric arrangement, its light falling with an exclusive optical selection. These things are a parable. The scratches are events, and the candle is the egoism of any person now absent – of Miss Vincy, for example. Rosamond had a Providence of her own who had kindly made her more charming than other girls, and who seemed to have arranged Fred's illness and Mr Wrench's mistake in order to bring her and Lydgate within effective proximity. It would have been to contravene these arrangements if Rosamond had consented to go away to Stone Court or elsewhere, as her parents wished her to do, especially since Mr Lydgate thought the precaution needless. Therefore, while Miss Morgan and the children were sent away to a farmhouse the morning after Fred's illness had declared itself, Rosamond refused to leave papa and mamma.

Poor mamma indeed was an object to touch any creature born of woman; and Mr Vincy, who doated on his wife, was more alarmed on her account than on Fred's. But for his insistence she would have taken no rest: her brightness was all bedimmed; unconscious of her costume which had always been so fresh and gay, she was like a sick bird with languid eye and plumage ruffled, her senses dulled to the sights and sounds that used most to interest her. Fred's delirium, in which he seemed to be wandering out of her reach, tore her heart. After her first outburst against Mr Wrench she went about very quietly: her one low cry was to Lydgate. She would follow him out of the room and put her hand on his arm moaning out,

'Save my boy.' Once she pleaded, 'He has always been good to me, Mr Lydgate: he never had a hard word for his mother,' – as if poor Fred's suffering were an accusation against him. All the deepest fibres of the mother's memory were stirred, and the young man whose voice took a gentler tone when he spoke to her, was one with the babe whom she had loved, with a love new to her, before he was born.

'I have good hope, Mrs Vincy,' Lydgate would say. 'Come down with me and let us talk about the food.' In that way he led her to the parlour where Rosamond was, and made a change for her, surprising her into taking some tea or broth which had been prepared for her. There was a constant understanding between him and Rosamond on these matters. He almost always saw her before going to the sick-room, and she appealed to him as to what she could do for mamma. Her presence of mind and adroitness in carrying out his hints were admirable, and it is not wonderful that the idea of seeing Rosamond began to mingle itself with his interest in the case.

This passage begins with an **epigraph** of the kind which heads each chapter. Each epigraph focuses our attention upon a particular issue which will feature in the following pages. Unlike the majority, this is not an attributed quotation, but was invented by George Eliot. It affirms that her concerns are with human events in history, rather than with the Olympian gods of Greek **myth**

It is a point to which she returns on the novel's last page, where she refers to the Christian saint Theresa, and the classical heroine Antigone. They were models of noble self-sacrifice, and Dorothea is regularly compared to both throughout *Middlemarch*. But at the end of the story the narrator laments that 'the medium in which their ardent deeds took shape is for ever gone' (p. 838). Eliot is committed to a **realist** mode of writing about the lives of ordinary human beings, rather than the exceptional creatures of myth and **legend**.

After the epigraph, the narrator alludes to a personal friend, an 'eminent philosopher'. The narrative voice assumes a human form at such points; it announces that it has a life beyond the telling of this story. It is tempting to identify the narrator with George Eliot, who knew prominent thinkers of the day, such as John Tyndall and Herbert Spencer. But it would be naive to overlook the artifice involved in composing the narrative voice, and it is difficult to identify it consistently with the author.

George Eliot's contemporaries would have assumed that the 'eminent philosopher' was a man. Philosophy, the domain of abstract thought, was conventionally masculine. Mention of the housemaid indicates that within a patriarchal society less elevated tasks, such as housework, are allocated to lower-class women.

George Eliot, going against the patriarchal grain, was fascinated by contemporary science and that interest furnished the striking image which follows. We are told that a lighted candle, placed against the surface of a mirror, will arrange haphazard scratches on that surface into a regular concentric pattern. Order emerges from chaos. But the effect is an illusion, created by 'exclusive optical selection'. The basic scientific experiment is then translated into terms of human understanding, and applied to the story being told. The scratches represent random events in the world; the candle represents a sentient being discerning pattern in the randomness. The self, (in this case Rosamond Vincy's self), perceives order, and acts in accordance with that perception. The truth is, however, that the order is illusory.

The word 'Providence' is introduced, as it frequently is in *Middlemarch*, to invoke the orthodox Christian view that God has an all-encompassing plan which grants meaning to the world. George Eliot, along with a significant number of other Victorian intellectuals, had lost faith in that divine provision. The word is used **ironically**, reducing it to the trivial status of a purely personal perception of order in the world: 'Rosamond had a Providence of her own who had kindly made her more charming than other girls'.

Casaubon's search for the key to all mythologies, and Lydgate's quest for the primitive tissue from which all others derive, may be seen as lighted candles placed against the scratched pier-glass of human existence. Both men wish to discover the sun around which the concentric circles have formed in their respective fields of study, to uncover the order which underpins their understanding. The **parable** offered here suggests that the sun is simply their own perception of pattern, not something detectable outside of themselves. They both labour under an illusion concerning the nature of human knowledge, and their failure is inevitable.

On a more mundane level, we can see that Rosamond's self-centredness precludes sympathy for others. Her brother's illness does not cause her great anxiety, but is a welcome occasion for her to exert influence over Lydgate. Her concern for her mother's well-being is, at least in part, motivated by her desire to make a favourable impression upon the doctor. It is not until her discussion with Dorothea in Chapter 82 that Rosamond learns to consider events from the point of view of another person. Only then does it become possible for her to extend sympathy.

Mrs Vincy's response to Fred's illness is dramatically different. Her son, in his early twenties, has caused disappointment and anxiety on account of his idleness and lack of direction. But now he 'was one with the babe whom she had loved, with a love new to her, before he was born'. Circumstances have transformed the mother's perception; tolerant affection has given way to an idealised vision. Evaluation of other people is always modified by changes in the emotional state of the perceiver. This is nowhere more evident than in the shift from Ladislaw's detached amusement at the prospect of Dorothea's marriage, in Chapter 9, to his later impassioned assessment of her as a perfect woman and a goddess descended to earth.

Middlemarch shows that the course of an individual life is unpredictable. It can be affected in a major way by events that might appear incidental to it. So, Fred Vincy's debts led him to travel to the horse-fair where he contracted fever. The Vincys were dissatisfied with Mr Wrench's treatment of their son, so Lydgate, who happened to be nearby, was summoned to attend him. Lydgate is attracted to Rosamond physically, and is impressed by her show of considerateness. They subsequently marry and his aspiration to accomplish important research is mired in the material demands of domestic life.

TEXT 2　　(PAGES 389–90)

'And you are going to engage Mr Garth, who praised my cottages, Sir James says.'

'Chettam is a little hasty, my dear,' said Mr Brooke, colouring slightly. 'A little hasty, you know. I never said I should do anything of the kind. I never said I should *not* do it, you know.'

'He only feels confident that you will do it,' said Dorothea, in a voice as clear and unhesitating as that of a young chorister chanting a *credo*, 'because you mean to enter Parliament as a member who cares for the improvement of the people, and one of the first things to be made better is the state of the land and the labourers. Think of Kit Downes, uncle, who lives with his wife and seven children in a house with one sitting-room and one bed-room hardly larger than this table! – and those poor Dagleys, in their tumble-down farmhouse, where they live in the back kitchen and leave the other rooms to the rats! That is one reason why I did not like the pictures here, dear uncle – which you think me stupid about. I used to come from the village with all that dirt and coarse ugliness like a pain within me, and the simpering pictures in the drawing-room seemed to me like a wicked attempt to find delight in what is false, while we don't mind how hard the truth is for the neighbours outside our walls. I think we have no right to come forward and urge wider changes for good, until we have tried to alter the evils which lie under our own hands.'

Dorothea had gathered emotion as she went on, and had forgotten everything except the relief of pouring forth her feelings, unchecked: an experience once habitual with her, but hardly ever present since her marriage, which had been a perpetual struggle of energy with fear. For the moment, Will's admiration was accompanied with a chilling sense of remoteness. A man is seldom ashamed of feeling that he cannot love a woman so well when he sees a certain greatness in her: nature having intended greatness for men. But nature has sometimes made sad oversights in carrying out her intentions; as in the case of good Mr Brooke, whose masculine consciousness was at this moment in rather a stammering condition under the eloquence of his niece. He could not immediately find any other mode of expressing himself than that of rising, fixing his eye-glass and fingering the papers before him. At last he said –

'There is something in what you say, my dear, something in what you say – but not everything – eh, Ladislaw. You and I don't like our pictures and statues being found fault with. Young ladies are a little ardent, you know – a little one-sided, my dear. Fine art, poetry, that kind of thing, elevates a nation – *emollit mores* – you understand a little Latin now. But – eh, what?'

These interrogatives were addressed to the footman who had come in to say that the keeper had found one of Dagley's boys with a leveret in his hand, just killed.

'I'll come, I'll come. I shall let him off easily, you know,' said Mr Brooke aside to Dorothea, shuffling away very cheerfully.

Dorothea is talking with her uncle, attempting to persuade him to make improvements in the living conditions of his tenants. She is aware that Brooke has been justly criticised for allowing his estate to deteriorate, while presenting himself as a reforming politician. She also sees an opportunity to realise at Tipton a plan for building cottages like those now built at Freshitt. Her altruism contrasts with his own limited vision, which is blinkered by self-interest.

Dorothea speaks with directness and fluency, which reflect her commitment. Indeed, she is compared to a choirboy singing a 'credo', a declaration of faith. The **simile** suggests her child-like innocence, and the religious passion which animates her very practical suggestions. Brooke, contrastingly, speaks with equivocation, unsure of his own position. His utterances are always far from fluent, displaying muddled thinking. He habitually includes the phrase 'you know', a verbal tic which soon becomes meaningless, while ostensibly referring to shared knowledge. It serves to emphasise Brooke's own debilitating lack of insight. His consciousness is reduced to 'a stammering condition under the eloquence of his niece'. George Eliot regularly uses contrast of this kind, developing characterisation by emphasising difference.

Dorothea is not only aware of the conditions endured by her uncle's tenants, she actually refers to those tenants by name. One of the themes of *Middlemarch* is the relationship between the general and the particular. Dorothea is devoted to ideas, and abides by general principles, but she also pays attention to specific details, showing sympathetic interest in particular cases. This grants her a moral astuteness which is not allowed by either principles or details alone. Later, Lydgate uses scientific terms to convey the need for such flexible vision: 'a man's mind must be continually expanding and shrinking between the whole human horizon and the horizon of an object-glass' (p. 640).

Dorothea is critical of the 'simpering pictures' her uncle favours. She criticises the 'wicked attempt to find delight in what is false' which they represent, in her view. George Eliot took pains to write responsible realist fiction, avoiding 'that softening influence of the fine arts which make other people's hardships picturesque' (p. 393). She was wary of dealing with issues that readers might find offensive, (her handling of Rigg's illegitimacy is notably cautious), but she is careful in *Middlemarch* to steer clear of sentimentality. She exposes hardships endured by the labouring class, but she does not idealise the farm workers.

Dorothea's marriage to Casaubon is described as 'a perpetual struggle of energy with fear' (p. 389). This is an abstract way to describe a woman's battle to overcome her sense of intimidation within a marriage, but it is a highly effective means of disclosing **epic** conflicts occurring beneath the surface of provincial life. Dorothea's frustration is in this way projected as a struggle conceived in terms that have universal significance. All human beings know fear, while energy is a basic requirement of existence.

Will Ladislaw is also present. He recognises 'a certain greatness' in Dorothea, which leaves him with 'a chilling sense of remoteness'. The narrator suggests that nature has 'intended greatness for men', adding with telling **irony** that in the case of Mr Brooke nature had failed in that intention. The irony undermines that sense of a natural order in which men are necessarily superior. The electoral speech Brooke later delivers is a disaster. That is not surprising given his lack of oratorical prowess. But Dorothea's persuasiveness and articulateness seem contrary to what was required of women in Victorian England, and Ladislaw is struck by the way she transcends the limits imposed by her gender. His high estimation of her is fuelled by admiration of that capacity to rise above her condition. Brooke's bumbling manner is endearing at the start of the novel, but it appears increasingly irresponsible and the product of selfishness. He patronises Dorothea, saying 'you understand a little Latin now'. She has conscientiously sought to compensate for her lack of classical education in order to do serious work with Casaubon. Brooke throws in a familiar Latin phrase which can scarcely be taken as proof of his own erudition. He suggests that young ladies are 'a little one-sided', but Dorothea's capacity to see things from more than one point of view contrasts starkly with his own incapacity to do so.

A footman arrives to announce that the gamekeeper has caught a poacher. The culprit is a member of the Dagley family to which Dorothea has just referred, and the crime is a clear indication of the hard times the family is experiencing. Brooke is a magistrate, accustomed to dealing with such transgressors. In Chapter 4 there is reference to 'poor Bunch', a sheep-stealer condemned to be hanged for his offence, despite Brooke's efforts to secure a pardon. He declares he will be lenient with young

Dagley. Brooke is essentially well-meaning, but tends to be insensitive and morally short-sighted.

TEXT 3   (PAGES 478–9)

Soon she could hear that he was sleeping, but there was no more sleep for her. While she constrained herself to lie still lest she should disturb him, her mind was carrying on a conflict in which imagination ranged its forces first on one side and then on the other. She had no presentiment that the power which her husband wished to establish over her future action had relation to anything else than his work. But it was clear enough to her that he would expect her to devote herself to sifting those mixed heaps of material, which were to be the doubtful illustration of principles still more doubtful. The poor child had become altogether unbelieving as to the trustworthiness of that Key which had made the ambition and the labour of her husband's life. It was not wonderful that, in spite of her small instruction, her judgment in this matter was truer than his: for she looked with unbiased comparison and healthy sense at probabilities on which he had risked all his egoism. And now she pictured to herself the days, and months, and years which she must spend in sorting what might be called shattered mummies, and fragments of a tradition which was itself a mosaic wrought from crushed ruins – sorting them as food for a theory which was already withered in the birth like an elfin child. Doubtless a vigorous error vigorously pursued has kept the embryos of truth a-breathing: the quest of gold being at the same time a questioning of substances, the body of chemistry is prepared for its soul, and Lavoisier is born. But Mr Casaubon's theory of the elements which made the seed of all tradition was not likely to bruise itself unawares against discoveries: it floated among flexible conjectures no more solid than those etymologies which seemed strong because of likeness in sound, until it was shown that likeness in sound made them impossible: it was a method of interpretation which was not tested by the necessity of forming anything which had sharper collisions than an elaborate notion of Gog and Magog: it was as free from interruption as a plan for threading the stars together. And Dorothea had so often had to check her weariness and impatience over this questionable riddle-guessing, as it revealed itself to her instead of the fellowship in high knowledge which was to make life worthier! She could understand well enough now why her husband had come to cling to her, as possibly the only hope left that his labours would ever take a shape in which they could be given to the world. At first it had seemed that he wished to keep even her aloof from any close knowledge of what he was doing; but gradually the terrible stringency of human need – the prospect of a too speedy death –

And here Dorothea's pity turned from her own future to her husband's past – nay, to his present hard struggle with a lot which had grown out of that past: the lonely labour, the ambition breathing hardly under the pressure of self-distrust; the goal receding, and the heavier limbs; and now at last the sword visibly trembling above him! And had she not wished to marry him that she might help him in his life's labour? – But she had thought the work was to be something greater, which she could serve devoutly for its own sake. Was it right, even to soothe his grief – would it be possible, even if she promised – to work as in a treadmill fruitlessly?

Casaubon, aware that his health is precarious, has asked Dorothea to continue his work in the event of his death. She has declined to commit herself, and has requested that he allow her until the following day to make a decision. He sleeps, but she lies awake, filled with dread at the prospect of a solitary life, engaged in labour which she now knows to be futile. Dorothea is torn between her sense of duty to Casaubon and his learning, and her desire to free herself from the obligation to pursue further his sterile work.

Twentieth-century novelists, such as Virginia Woolf (1882–1941) and James Joyce (1882–1941), pioneered techniques of **interior monologue**, which granted readers direct access to the thoughts of a character. The conventions of the nineteenth-century **realist** novel did not permit such bold entry into the workings of an individual consciousness, but George Eliot manages to render the conflict in Dorothea's mind through the voice of her **omniscient narrator**.

That voice reports Dorothea's inner turmoil, while also indicating the limits of her understanding. It remarks that 'she had no presentiment that the power which her husband wished to establish over her future action had relation to anything else than his work'. This unilluminating comment assumes considerable significance following her husband's death, when it is revealed that a codicil added to his will prohibits her marriage to Will Ladislaw as long as she remains owner of Lowick Manor.

At this point, the observation does indicate that exercise of power over his wife is the essence of Casaubon's view of his marriage. In fact, desire for power over another human being is evident in many other social relationships in *Middlemarch*, from Featherstone's persistent humiliation of Fred Vincy to Raffles's attempts to extort money from Bulstrode. In such a context, the aspirations of idealistic individuals inevitably encounter prolonged struggle.

Dorothea is described as a 'poor child', reminding us that she is still only in her early twenties, but also indicating the position of subordination and dependency in which she found herself as a married woman in a patriarchal society. She entered into marriage with the impression that her husband inhabited an enchanted land of learning and wisdom. Now she recognises that his work will offer only 'doubtful illustration of principles still more doubtful'. She has become a sceptic, 'altogether unbelieving as to the trustworthiness of that Key which had made the ambition and the labour of her husband's life'.

This is personal disillusionment, but it also registers the scepticism which by the 1870s, when George Eliot was writing, had become the hallmark of the age. She became sceptical about religion in the early 1840s. But her reading and the company she kept exposed her to doubt as a crucial element in contemporary philosophy and science. The Key to All Mythologies for which Casaubon searches is a conception of truth in which late Victorian intellectuals had lost belief. Similarly, Lydgate's quest for the primitive tissue from which all others were derived is misguided, in George Eliot's view.

Dorothea has had the limited education allowed to a woman, but despite this 'small instruction' she is sufficiently clear-sighted to recognise the role of Casaubon's 'egoism' in determining the course of his research (see the image of the pier-glass, discussed in Textual Analysis: Text 1). Her husband's legacy to her is a heap of fragments, which are to be pieced together to conform to a discredited theory.

The generalities with which human knowledge has sought to give shape to the particulars of experience have changed throughout history. Theories current in one age have been superseded in the next. Laws which once seemed immutable have proven to be inadequate to changing circumstances. This is the picture of human understanding which George Eliot gives here, with her references to the alchemist's 'quest for gold', which gave way to Lavoisier's modern chemistry. Casaubon's theory exists in a more rarefied atmosphere, like 'a plan for threading the stars together'. It is 'a method of interpretation' which has become obsolete. The point of view of the age has changed.

Dorothea has been disappointed in her hope of finding 'the fellowship in high knowledge which was to make life worthier'. Yet her sympathetic nature can still extend pity to the man who seeks to control her life even after his death. The questions asked in the concluding paragraph of this passage are examples of a technique called **free indirect style**. The third-person voice is still present, but it implies the first person. These are questions which Dorothea asks herself, but they are not presented directly. In **interior monologue**, the question 'And had she not wished to marry him that she might help him in his life's labours?' would appear as, 'Did I not wish to marry him in order to help him with his life's labours?'. Free indirect style allows George Eliot to filter the question through the voice of her **omniscient narrator**

PART FIVE

BACKGROUND

GEORGE ELIOT

'George Eliot' was the assumed name of Mary Ann Evans, who was born on 22 November 1819, at South Farm, Arbury, in Warwickshire. Her father, Robert Evans, managed the estate of Francis Newdigate. Her mother, Christiana Pearson, was Evans's second wife. Mary Ann had an older sister and brother, Christiana and Isaac.

Soon after her birth, the family moved to Griff House, on another part of the estate. Mary Ann started school in 1824. Her formal education continued until 1836, when her mother's illness and subsequent death brought it to an end. The following year she assumed the role of housekeeper to her father, but through her own efforts, and by arranging further lessons with tutors from Coventry, she continued to study Greek, Latin, Italian, French and German.

As a child, Mary Ann was ardently religious. In 1840 her faith remained strong and she published a poem in the *Christian Observer*. Then, in 1841, she and her father moved to Coventry, enabling Isaac to take over Griff House, following his marriage. She entered a circle of sceptics and freethinkers, and early in 1842 her refusal to attend church resulted in temporary estrangement from her father. She remained a sceptic and agnostic throughout the rest of her life, yet was interested in controversial works of contemporary theology. In January 1844, she began a translation from German of David Strauss's *The Life of Jesus*, eventually published anonymously in 1846. In 1845 she received a proposal of marriage from a picture-restorer, whose name is not known.

In 1849 her father died, leaving her a small guaranteed income for the rest of her life. She travelled in Europe, with her liberal friends Charles and Cara Bray. At this time, she changed her name to 'Marianne', then 'Marian'. In 1850, she contributed her first article to the *Westminster Review*. In September 1851, she became its assistant editor, mingling with the leading thinkers of the day. She developed a close friendship with the philosopher, Herbert Spencer (1820–1903). In October 1851, she first encountered George Henry Lewes (1817–78), writer, philosopher, and scientist. They fell in love, but Lewes was already married, and although separated from his wife, he was unable to secure a divorce. Nonetheless, Lewes and Evans lived together as husband and wife. It was a bold decision, considered immoral by most people at that time. Her brother had no further contact with her until after Lewes's death.

In 1854, Mary Ann Evans's translation of Ludwig Feuerbach's controversial study *The Essence of Christianity* was published. In July she travelled to Germany, where Lewes worked on his *Life of Goethe* and she wrote articles. On their return to London in 1855, they continued to live together, gradually winning acceptance for that arrangement. By 1877, their social prestige was such that they dined with Princess Louise. Lewes died in November 1878.

On 6 May 1880, Evans surprised her friends by marrying J.W. ('Johnny') Cross, an American banker, more than twenty years her junior. Shortly after moving with him to central London, she fell ill, and on 22 December she died from pneumonia, aged 61 years. She is buried in Highgate Cemetery, North London, alongside G.H. Lewes.

In 1885, J.W. Cross published *George Eliot's Life: As Related in Her Letters and Journals*. Cross edited the materials carefully to ensure that his late wife appeared conventionally virtuous. The result is a very partial portrait, and some who knew her remarked that it made her seem dull, which in life she never was.

Eliot's *Letters*, edited by G.S. Haight, were published in nine volumes by Oxford University Press, between 1954 and 1978. Haight's *George Eliot: A Biography* (Oxford University Press, 1968) has long been regarded as the standard biographical work. An important recent biography is Frederick Karl's *George Eliot* (HarperCollins, 1995).

OTHER WORKS

In 1857, the stories collected as *Scenes of Clerical Life* began to appear in *Blackwood's Magazine*. It was at this time that she took the pseudonym, 'George Eliot'. The name change may have been partly defensive, concealing the authorship of Mary Ann Evans, (now calling herself Marian), who was living scandalously with George Lewes. But there seems to have been a conscious decision to lay claim to the authority reserved for men in a patriarchal society, and to circumvent the assumptions which awaited fiction written by a woman. She did, of course, write as a woman, but increasingly with a seriousness conventionally considered masculine.

Her fiction grew increasingly challenging and complex, culminating in *Middlemarch*, her **epic** of provincial life, and her sophisticated novel of Jewish culture, *Daniel Deronda* (1876). The earlier novels *Adam Bede* (1859), *The Mill on the Floss* (1860), and *Silas Marner* (1861) are more immediately accessible, but they establish some of her enduring concerns. In *Adam Bede*, her commitment to literary **realism** was already clear, in a portrait of rural English life which explores the nature of human sympathy. *The Mill on the Floss* anticipates *Middlemarch* in its account of the effect of the narrowness of provincial life upon young people with aspirations. *Silas Marner* is also a tale of dreams and disillusionment.

Her travels in Europe broadened George Eliot's horizons and furnished material for her historical novel, *Romola* (1863), which is set in Italy. In *Middlemarch* she combined Roman episodes with her study of the English Midlands at the time of the first Reform Act. *Felix Holt, the Radical* (1866) is focused on those political issues, leading to the passing of the Act in 1832, as they reverberate through ordinary lives. George Eliot's fiction sustains a remarkable level of achievement, but *Middlemarch* is widely held to be her creative peak.

HISTORICAL BACKGROUND

Middlemarch was written between 1869 and 1871, but the story is set in the years 1829 to 1832. The intervening period had wrought significant changes in the nature of English society, and had witnessed more fundamental changes in the way the world was understood by scientists and philosophers. An important critical distance is established by those forty years separating the fictional action from the actual writing of the novel. It enabled George Eliot to indicate to her initial readers ongoing processes of social change.

REFORM

By 1815, Parliament had sanctioned the enclosure of common land, extending the property rights of wealthy landowners while dispossessing those who had previously farmed the open fields. Some became tenant farmers dependent for their well-being upon the conscience of a landowner. In *Middlemarch*, we can see that those at Freshitt benefit from Chettam's enlightened view, while others, like Dagley who lives and works on Brooke's land, are less fortunate. Labourers experienced terrible poverty, and sometimes responded with violent protest, including the burning of crops. Others lapsed into theft; the case of a man sentenced to be hanged for stealing a sheep is mentioned in Chapter 4.

Increasingly during the years leading to the period depicted in *Middlemarch*, agricultural workers were leaving the countryside and moving to towns where they found employment in manufacturing industries, such as the company that Vincy owns. Their working conditions were often appalling. Mrs Cadwallader vitriolically refers to Vincy as 'one of those who suck the life out of the wretched handloom weavers of Tipton and Freshitt' (p. 327). The arrival of the railway accelerated this movement from country to town, transforming the basis of the English economy from agriculture to industry. The process of rural depopulation resulted in a drift of social power and influence, away from the upper classes towards members of the middle classes such as Nicholas Bulstrode.

A significant imbalance soon became evident in parliamentary representation. Rapidly expanding industrial towns, and even cities like Birmingham and Manchester, were unrepresented, while rural regions retained their traditional enfranchisement. There persisted in these regions 'rotten boroughs', which returned a member to Parliament despite being almost uninhabited, and 'pocket boroughs' where voting was controlled by a single landowner. Electoral corruption and inequality is discussed in the opening pages of Chapter 37.

The First Reform Act, promoted by the Prime Minister Lord Grey and his Home Secretary Lord John Russell, became law in June 1832. It reformed the electoral system, enabling the middle classes to participate much more extensively in government. Still, the working class and a substantial proportion of the lower middle class remained unenfranchised. It was not until 1867 that Benjamin Disraeli's Second Reform Act extended voting rights to working class men in towns and cities. Agricultural workers had to await the Third Reform Act, in 1884–5. Women of all classes were excluded from the franchise until the twentieth century.

RELIGION

There are numerous references in *Middlemarch* to 'the Catholic question'. Roman Catholics were excluded from public office, from university education, and from commissions in the armed forces.

The Anglican monopoly of positions of power, institutionalised through the Test and Corporations Acts, also excluded dissenting Protestants. In 1829, the Whig politician Lord John Russell pushed a bill through Parliament repealing the Acts. Advantages were extended to dissenters, but not to Roman Catholics, a relatively small group in England. In Ireland the majority of the population were Catholics, and they protested energetically at being excluded from any form of political representation. Sir Robert Peel, Home Secretary in the Tory government led by the Duke of Wellington, passed the Roman Catholic Relief Act in 1829, granting Catholics the same rights as the Protestant dissenters.

The aristocracy and landed gentry, such as Chettam and Brooke, belonged to the Church of England. Many of those engaged in commerce were dissenting Protestants. It is a measure of Bulstrode's acquired social power, as well as of his hypocrisy, that after many years as a committed non-conformist, he has changed his allegiance to the established Anglican church. Note that Brooke had an ancestor who was 'a Puritan gentleman who served under Cromwell, but afterwards conformed, and managed to come out of all political troubles as the proprietor of a respectable family estate' (p. 7).

Dorothea belongs to the Anglican establishment, and she marries a clergyman, yet she 'had been brought up in English and Swiss Puritanism, fed on meagre Protestant histories' (p. 193). Non-conformity is manifested in her determined individualism; she follows her own conscience, rather than being circumscribed by the accepted view. She speaks of her own flexibility in religion: 'whenever I find one way that makes it a wider blessing than any other, I cling to that as the truest – I

mean that which takes in the most good of all kinds, and brings in the
most people as sharers in it' (p. 495).

The narrator refers disparagingly to low-church intolerance of any
form of sensual indulgence: 'The Vincys had the readiness to enjoy, the
rejection of all anxiety, and the belief in life as a merry lot, which made a
house exceptional in most county towns at that time, when
Evangelicalism had cast a certain suspicion as of a plague-infection over
the few amusements which had survived in the provinces' (p. 161). Such
observations feed into the novel a sense of the historical realities of the
period.

Importantly, George Eliot shows Christianity to be a belief that
encompasses divergent points of view, rather than being the monolithic
authority it had been during the European middle ages. The existence of
variant interpretations in all fields of human understanding is one of the
major thematic concerns in *Middlemarch*. Reference to reforms extending
rights to non-Anglicans also reflects the novel's concern with the
possibility of social change. If reform in terms of both class and religion
could occur, then modification of the status of women was also
conceivable.

LOSS OF FAITH

In the *British Quarterly Review* in 1873, R.H. Hutton foresaw that
future critics would see *Middlemarch* 'as registering the low-tide mark of
spiritual belief among the literary class in the nineteenth century'.

Throughout her adult life, George Eliot was an agnostic, unable to
sustain belief in orthodox religious doctrines. In this respect, her
experience was typical of many middle class intellectuals of the Victorian
period. Her early faith was eroded by her exposure to the arguments of
scientific rationalism and to critical readings of the Bible offered by
contemporary progressive scholarship. The years 1829–32, in which
Middlemarch is set, correspond closely to the critical time in her own
response to Christian orthodoxy.

The narrator of *Middlemarch* observes that 'scepticism, as we know,
can never be thoroughly applied, else life would come to a standstill:
something we must believe in and do' (p. 240). Dorothea's belief is 'That
by desiring what is perfectly good, even when we don't quite know what

it is and cannot do what we would, we are part of the divine power against evil – widening the skirts of light and making the struggle with darkness narrower' (p. 392). George Eliot appears to have espoused a secular version of this faith.

The evolutionary theory of Charles Darwin (1809–82) fuelled what Hutton called the 'great wave of scepticism', as it appeared to discredit the Biblical account of Creation. But making a positive variation on Darwinian theory, *Middlemarch* suggests that although individuals may fail to meet their aspirations, the gradual evolution of human society is served by that personal vision which does not merely settle for the way things are in the present. What remained unsettling for many of her contemporaries was the diminished role within this process of the individual life.

THE MEDICAL PROFESSION

Medical education underwent substantial change during the course of the nineteenth century. A new training school at University College London opened in 1828. Other London hospitals established medical schools during the 1830s. Most medical education at that point was provided by established practitioners, replicating their methods. The General Medical Council came into being in 1858 to control qualifications and, increasingly, to regularise practice.

George Eliot reflects contemporary debates surrounding treatment and diagnosis. Lydgate's qualifications, his theories and his practice are all points of contention. He runs into conflict with Sprague and Minchin, the established practitioners for the region. They have been authorised by the Royal College of Physicians, an institution for which Lydgate has little time. They are disturbed that he does not conform to the pattern of the surgeon-apothecary which had been continued by Mr Peacock his predecessor, and is reflected in the approach of Mr Wrench.

Lydgate's modern outlook is shown in his use of a stethoscope, which was by no means common practice at that time. He is inspired by Vesalius, founder of modern anatomy, and by the French physiologist, Bichat, and he views the new hospital not merely as a place to tend the sick, but as a centre for research. Popular misapprehension is exemplified by Mrs Dollop, landlady of the Tankard inn, who speculates that Lydgate may allow patients to die in order to anatomise their dead bodies (p. 442).

LITERARY BACKGROUND

HENRY FIELDING

In Chapter 15, the narrator alludes to 'a great historian', who has taken 'his place amongst the colossi whose huge legs our living pettiness is observed to walk under' (p. 141). The reference is to Henry Fielding (1707–54), a writer who set the course the English novel would take for a hundred years. His great work, *Tom Jones* (1749), is comparable to *Middlemarch* in its scope and technical achievement, although the England it depicts is markedly different. One reason for the allusion is to draw our attention to historical change. George Eliot's novel portrays the arrival of a more hurried and money-driven society.

Her narrator refers especially to Fielding's tendency to indulge in 'copious remarks and digressions' (p. 141), making direct address to his readers. He made no attempt to conceal his own voice as it delivered moral guidance, drawing large conclusions applicable to the world as a whole. *Middlemarch* follows his example in its use of an **omniscient narrator**, passing comment on the action of the novel, but it would be wrong to identify this narrator as a firmly didactic authorial voice of the kind Fielding employed.

The narrative voice in *Middlemarch* is less assured and less consistent. It is omniscient in the sense that it assumes access to characters' thoughts, and can report separate events occurring simultaneously, but its interpretations always imply that another point of view is possible. George Eliot's narrator concludes: 'I at least have so much to do in unravelling certain human lots, and seeing how they were woven and interwoven, that all the light I can command must be concentrated on this particular web, and not dispersed over that tempting range of relevancies called the universe' (p. 141). The capacity to pass judgement with absolute confidence has been lost.

THE NINETEENTH-CENTURY NOVEL

From the point of view of the literary historian, the novel in the early years of the nineteenth century was dominated by the **social satires** of Jane Austen (1775–1817) and the **historical novels** of Sir Walter Scott (1771–1832). In Victorian England, William Makepeace Thackeray (1811–63), Charles Dickens (1812–70), and Anthony Trollope (1815–82) achieved great popular success with their novels portraying modern manners or addressing pressing issues of the day in an entertaining fashion. Their achievement was considerable, but elsewhere the novel was being conceived as a more self-consciously serious form of literary art.

Gustave Flaubert (1821–80) raised the French novel to a new level of refinement. The sophisticated Russian writer Ivan Turgenev (1818–83), who paid regular visits to George Eliot's home, achieved a comparable degree of seriousness. Such elevated aspirations entered the English tradition with the later work of George Eliot, signalling the way for developments in fiction in the early decades of the twentieth century. The 'formidable' presence George Eliot consequently became within the tradition of writing by women has been provocatively assessed by Elaine Showalter, in *A Literature of Their Own* (London: Virago, 1978).

PART SIX

CRITICAL HISTORY & BROADER PERSPECTIVES

RECEPTION AND EARLY CRITICAL VIEWS

Middlemarch first appeared in 1871–2. George Eliot had at that time established a reputation as England's leading novelist. The novel was eagerly anticipated, and expectation was heightened by the initial publication in parts at intervals. Literary magazines reviewed the parts as they appeared, caught up in the tensions of the unfolding plot.

Upon completion, George Eliot's friend Edith Simcox wrote an insightful review in the *Academy* in January 1873, noting the author's sustained focus on the 'inner life' of her characters, with events in the external world serving to support extended investigation of 'mental experience'. She also remarked upon parallels between Lydgate and Dorothea.

Henry James, who later became a major novelist, described *Middlemarch* as 'a treasure house of details', but 'an indifferent whole'. He found Ladislaw insubstantial, yet admired the portrayal of Lydgate, and approved of George Eliot's judicious handling of Casaubon's 'hollow pretentiousness and mouldy egotism'.

There was immediate critical uneasiness at the novel's pessimism, especially the absence of Christian consolation. R.H. Hutton, in the *Spectator*, admired the broad and accurate portrayal of provincial life, but commented on the novel's 'melancholy scepticism' and noted 'a certain air of moral desolation'. This perception of a basis for despair in her work contributed to a decline in George Eliot's popular and critical reputation from the end of the nineteenth century until the middle of the twentieth. In *The Cornhill Magazine*, in 1881, Leslie Stephen described *Middlemarch* as 'a rather painful book', and other readers around the turn of the century, including George Bernard Shaw, found it excessively analytical and insufficiently optimistic.

George Eliot's reputation declined during the 1890s, and her earlier, less ambitious novels were far more widely read and discussed than *Middlemarch* and other later works, until the middle of the twentieth century. In 1919, 100 years after George Eliot's birth, Virginia Woolf wrote an essay for the *Times Literary Supplement* which identified *Middlemarch* as the pinnacle of her achievement. But this view was not generally promoted until the influential Cambridge academic F.R. Leavis made the case for the novel's centrality to English literary history in *The Great Tradition* (1948).

Joan Bennett's *George Eliot: Her Mind and Her Art* was also published in 1948. Bennett stressed the importance of location. *Middlemarch* was Eliot's masterpiece because it brought her accumulated command of novelistic skills to bear on a region of England she knew intimately. The appearance of G.S. Haight's edition of George Eliot's letters during the 1950s gave added impetus to the renewed critical interest.

Barbara Hardy's *The Novels of George Eliot: A Study in Form* (1959) is an important work in the history of George Eliot criticism. Hardy traced the intricate patterning by means of which the novelist gave form to the copious materials of her fiction. The study refuted Henry James's claim that *Middlemarch* lacked overall control. W.J. Harvey's *The Art of George Eliot* (1961) also placed emphasis upon formal organisation.

Jerome Beaty's *Middlemarch: From Notebook to Novel*, published in 1960, was a scholarly investigation into the compositional process, unravelling the order of writing and of revising this large book. He draws on the author's preparatory planning for the novel, which had been published in 1950 as the *Quarry for 'Middlemarch'*, edited by A.T. Kitchel. In *A Critical History of English Literature* (1960), David Daiches argued that George Eliot introduced a new seriousness into the English novel. Prior to her work the genre had been primarily entertainment, but she promoted moral and intellectual sophistication. *Middlemarch*, he found 'one of the very greatest of English novels', especially notable for its 'complex network of interrelationships'.

Publication of G.S. Haight's *George Eliot: A Biography*, in 1968, stimulated criticism based in biography. Another documentary resource, a collection of George Eliot's essays, edited by Thomas Pinney, had appeared in 1963.

Critical evaluations of George Eliot, and of *Middlemarch*, have been conveniently collected in *A Century of George Eliot Criticism* (Methuen, 1966), edited by G.S. Haight, *George Eliot: The Critical Heritage* (Routledge, 1971) edited by David Carroll, and the 'Casebook' *George Eliot: Middlemarch*, edited by Patrick Swinden (Macmillan, 1972).

Since the 1970s, George Eliot's work has been subjected to a range of contemporary critical approaches, including structuralism, Bahktinian analysis, and deconstruction. Feminist critics in particular have found her fiction a fertile arena for debate.

In 1979, the year before the centenary of her death, Hugh Witemeyer considered the novels in relation to other art forms in *George Eliot and the Visual Arts* (Yale University Press). Beryl Gray examined the novelist's engagement with music in *George Eliot and Music* (Macmillan, 1989). Sally Shuttleworth looked at the fiction in another cultural context in *George Eliot and Nineteenth-Century Science* (Cambridge University Press, 1984).

CONTEMPORARY APPROACHES

NEW HISTORICISM

New Historicism is not a narrow method but a broad approach to reading texts. The New Historicist critic aligns the literary work with other documents from the period, and by considering them together discloses social forces in operation. The writer may have been unaware of these forces, but they may nonetheless have shaped the composition of the text.

Middlemarch is clearly caught up in an ongoing debate on education. Rosamond Vincy is educated to be a decorative young lady, and although Dorothea Brooke's education is more substantial it still imposes severe limitations on her understanding of the ways of the world. Fred Vincy and Christy Garth both receive a university education, conventionally a necessity for the social advancement of young men. From 1869, Girton College, situated in Hitchin, mid-way between London and Cambridge, offered more advanced education for young women. George Eliot made a financial contribution to its founding, although she was not unequivocal in her support for its aims.

A biographical critic might use her letters on the subject to cast light on the novel's handling of educational issues. A New Historicist critic would not feel bound to look for such personal materials, but might draw, for example, upon the documentation surrounding Forster's Education Act which was passed by Parliament in 1870, the year before publication of *Middlemarch* began. The Act, which extended elementary education to all, meant an increase in the general level of literacy. It was surrounded by a mass of well-documented argument. The novel might be read in relation to that discourse, and the critic might consider the implications of the fact that George Eliot was writing, at that time, a challenging, philosophically serious novel, which would pose a daunting prospect for a reading public that was about to grow rapidly.

Medical knowledge is also an evident concern of *Middlemarch*. Lydgate promotes a new understanding of the human body and is met with a largely hostile reaction. A New Historicist might collate documents elucidating advances in nineteenth-century medicine, and then consider how new models offered by anatomy and physiology may be considered in relation to George Eliot's representation of human beings in her novel.

The **metaphor** of the web, which Lydgate admires in the work of the physiologist Bichat, assumes considerable structural and thematic importance in *Middlemarch*. It was a familiar metaphor in nineteenth-century scientific thought, including the work of Charles Darwin. Important studies which may be said to assume a New Historicist orientation are Sally Shuttleworth's *George Eliot and Nineteenth-Century Science* (Cambridge University Press, 1984) and Gillian Beer's *Darwin's Plots* (Routledge, 1983).

FEMINIST CRITICISM

The term 'feminist criticism' covers a range of approaches crucially concerned with the representation of women, their personal identities, and their social relationships within a society dominated by men. A woman writer who assumed a man's name when publishing her work might be expected to exercise a particular fascination for feminist critics, but they have been divided in their response to George Eliot's work.

George Eliot was unconventional, even radical, in the way she lived her own life, but her creation Dorothea Brooke becomes the self-sacrificing Mrs Casaubon, and after that chastening experience she surrenders herself to the requirements of being Mrs Ladislaw, wife and mother. Some critics have found that *Middlemarch* reproduces the dominant assumptions of patriarchal society, with no significant reversal of gender roles, and with the conventionally feminine virtue of passive compliance endorsed as a positive quality.

Middlemarch begins, admittedly, with reference to the willing martyrdom of Saint Theresa, but there are arguably important **ironies** being overlooked in this reading, and it is possible to discern a more actively feminist voice in the novel. For example, our attention is repeatedly drawn to the artificiality of Rosamond Vincy's training as a feminine woman, and although she appears obstinately childish and selfish, it is not difficult to make a case that she is a victim of patriarchal gender construction.

Rosamond has been manufactured as a social ornament, and has become an apparently insubstantial snob. But if her appearance did not conform to the prevalent definition of beauty, and if her parents were not so concerned for their children to become more elevated socially, she might have directed her intelligence and energies to more constructive ends. In their important feminist study *The Madwoman in the Attic* (Yale University Press, 1979), Sandra Gilbert and Susan Gubar identify Rosamond Vincy as George Eliot's most important rebellious female, and argue that when she and Dorothea have their emotional encounter near the end of *Middlemarch*, they seem childish because their full maturity has been denied by imposed femininity.

Gillian Beer, in *George Eliot* (Harvester Press, 1980) also makes the case that Rosamond was entrapped by patriarchal views. She surveys earlier feminist work on George Eliot, and affirms that although she was not a militant participant in the woman's movement she was aware of the key issues of contemporary debate, and fed them into *Middlemarch*. Jennifer Uglow, in *George Eliot* (Virago, 1987) finds her a more tentative feminist, who endorsed the perpetuation of certain established female values, and was ambivalent towards organised feminism.

POST-STRUCTURALIST CRITICISM

About thirty years ago, an array of theoretical positions became apparent, primarily in French academic discourse, which has become known as post-structuralism. These diverse theories have in common a disregard for the intentions of the author, and an emphasis upon the play of language within a text. The post-structuralist critic is not interested in what George Eliot wanted her novel to signify. Rather, the focus is upon signification itself, and its inherent instability.

In other words, not only is *Middlemarch* not governed by George Eliot's intention, but structures of meaning within the language of the text are themselves flawed in crucial ways, leading to inconsistencies which the post-structuralist takes to be inevitable, given the nature of language. One of the prominent manifestations of post-structuralism is deconstruction, a critical practice which takes its lead from the work of the French philosopher Jacques Derrida (b. 1930). Deconstruction exposes texts breaking the laws they claim to abide by.

A distinguished demonstration of this form of criticism is *Blindness and Insight* by Paul De Man (Oxford University Press, 1971). In a broad application of De Man's approach, we might return to the passage used for Textual Analysis One. That passage presents an image of a pier-glass, or mirror, which is covered with haphazard scratches. The narrator remarks that if you place a lighted candle against it, the scratches appear to form themselves into a series of concentric circles. It is the candle which produces the illusion of concentric arrangement, through a process of optical selection. This is a **metaphor** which suggests that events assume the semblance of order through the action of the perceiver or interpreter, rather than being intrinsically ordered.

This insight discloses the importance of point of view in *Middlemarch*. Instead of reality being a self-evident order of truth, it now appears to be the product of multiple interpretations, overlapping but never identical. Individual egos preside over concentric circles of meaning, but these are not contained within an overall unitary order, and consequently characters clash in their view of things and are often troubled by mutual misunderstanding. Following De Man's example, we might point out George Eliot's inconsistency in deploying an **omniscient narrator** to furnish this insight.

Preserving the all-knowing voice, she sought to hold together a fictional world that is inherently fragmented. We might say that she sought to affirm the presence of God, despite her avowed agnosticism. It might also be shown that the identity of this omniscient narrator is less unified than it initially appears. Not only are there apparent inconsistencies in its observations, but the voice itself assumes at times a markedly different character, which might be taken to register internal divisions. Nonetheless, the semblance of omniscience is preserved in a way which is discredited by the metaphor of the candle and the mirror.

A sophisticated deconstructive reading can be found in J. Hillis Miller's 'Optic and semiotic in Middlemarch', in *The Worlds of Victorian Fiction*, edited by Jerome Buckley (Harvard University Press, 1975).

World events	Author's life	Literary events

1866

| War between Austria and Prussia; Russell ministry resigns after defeat of Reform Bill; Derby forms Conservative ministry with Disraeli as leader of the House of Commons | *Felix Holt, The Radical* published | Carlyle, *On the Choice of Books;* Dostoevsky, *Crime and Punishment;* Gaskell, *Wives and Daughters;* Rossetti, C., *The Prince's Progress and other Poems* |

1867

| Second Reform Bill passed by Parliament, adding nearly one million to the electorate; Fenian rising in Ireland; USA buys Alaska from Russia; Lister's use of carbolic antiseptic reduces risk of infection in surgery; Nobel patents dynamite | Travels around Spain with G.H. Lewes | Arnold, *On the Study of Celtic Literature; New Poems;* Marx, *Das Kapital;* Ruskin, *Time and Tide;* Tolstoy, *War and Peace* (completed 1869) |

1868

| Gladstone becomes Liberal Prime Minister; first annual Trade Union Congress in Manchester | Returns from Spain and begins to live with G.H. Lewes as his wife; *The Spanish Gypsy* published | Alcott, *Little Women;* Queen Victoria, *Leaves from a Journal of Our Life in the Highlands;* Browning, *The Ring and the Book* |

1869

| Anglican Church disestablished in Ireland; Suez Canal opened; first transcontinental American railway completed; *Cutty Sark* launched | *Agatha: A Poem* published; work on a story about a provincial town called Middlemarch begins; second son of G.H.Lewes, Thornie, dies | Arnold, *Culture and Anarchy; Collected Poems;* Blackmore, *Lorna Doone;* Flaubert, *Sentimental Education;* Mill, *On the Subjection of Women;* Tennyson, *The Holy Grail, and Other Poems* |

World events	Author's life	Literary events
1870 Outbreak of the Franco-Prussian War (–1871); siege of Paris; Gladstone's first Irish Land Act passed; first Married Women's Property Act gives wives right to keep their earnings; diamond mining starts in South Africa; death of Charles Dickens	The first ten chapters of *Middlemarch*, as we know it, are written	**1870** Dickens, *The Mystery of Edwin Drood; Speeches, Literary and Social;* Disraeli, *Lothair;* Huxley, T.H., *Sermons, Addresses and Reviews;* Ruskin, *Lectures on Art;* Verne, *Twenty Thousand Leagues under the Sea;* Swinburne, *Ode on the Proclamation of a French Republic*
1871 Prussia victorious over France; Paris Commune supressed; in Britain, Trade Union Act makes picketing illegal; bill passed abolishing religious tests at Oxford and Cambridge Universities allowing attendance by non-Anglicans; Darwin, *The Descent of Man*	The story set in Middlemarch begun in 1869 and the story of Miss Brooke written in 1870 are married together to form *Middlemarch;* in December the first part of *Middlemarch* is published	**1871** Lewis Carroll, *Through the Looking Glass;* Meredith, *The Adventures of Harry Richmond;* Ruskin, *Fors Calvigera; Letters to the Workmen and Labourers of Great Britain;* Lear, *Nonsense Songs and Stories*
1872 Ballot Act secures secret voting; National Labourers' Union founded; Monet, *Impression, Sunrise*	*Middlemarch* is a commercial and critical success; in December a four-volume edition of the work is published	**1872** Hardy, *Under the Greenwood Tree;* Nietzsche, *The Birth of Tragedy;* Browning, R., *Fifine at the Fair;* Lear, *More Nonsense Songs;* Tennyson, *Gareth and Lynette*

World events	Author's life	Literary events
1873 Agricultural and financial depression starts throughout Britain; first commercially successful typewriter designed in America; invention of barbed wire in America	'Guinea Edition' of *Middlemarch* published in March	**1873** Arnold, *Literature and Dogma;* Hardy, *A Pair of Blue Eyes;* Spencer, *The Study of Sociology;* Browning, R., *Red Cotton Night-Cap Country*
1874 Disraeli becomes Conservative PM (–1880); Building Societies Act encourages home ownership	*The Legend of Jubal and Other Poems* published; serialisation of *Daniel Deronda* begun	**1874** Hardy, *Far From the Madding Crowd;* Ruskin, *Val d'Arno;* Wordsworth, D., *Recollections of a Tour Made in Scotland*
1875 Social reforms of Disraeli's administration include Public Health Act, Artisans' Dwelling Act and Sale of Food and Drugs Act; Disraeli buys Britain shares in the Suez Canal; completion of London's main drainage system	*Daniel Deronda* continues to be serialised, and George Eliot is now firmly recognised as the greatest living English novelist	**1875** Arnold, *God and the Bible;* Trollope, *The Way We Live Now;* Browning R., *Aristophanes' Apology;* *The Inn Album;* Morris, *The Aeneid of Virgil* (trans.), Tennyson, *The Lover's Tale*
1876 Merchant Shipping Act adopts Plimsoll's load-line for ships; Bell invents the modern telephone; Bissell invents the carpet sweeper; the ammonium refrigerator invented; Otto invents four-stroke gas engine	The serialisation of *Daniel Deronda* ends, and the novel is published in volume form	**1876** Bradley, F.H., *Ethical Studies;* Hardy, *The Hand of Ethelberta;* James, *Roderick Hudson;* Spencer, *The Principles of Sociology;* Mark Twain, *The Adventures of Tom Sawyer*

dialect manner of speaking a language, particular to a locality

epic long narrative work which aspires to encompass all aspects of an epoch or a nation

epigraph a quotation placed at the start of a literary work to focus attention on the meaning of what follows

flashback term taken from cinema, signifying a sudden jump back to an earlier episode or scene

free indirect style a blend of third- and first-person narrative, which in effect filters the thoughts of a character through the voice of a narrator

historical novel a fiction set in the past, mingling real and imaginary characters

interior monologue a technique for rendering the flow of thoughts within a character's mind

irony the quality of an utterance or an event which appears to signify one thing but in fact conveys a meaning other than the obvious

legend story about a heroic figure

melodrama writing which relies upon sensational happenings, violent action, and improbable events

metaphor one thing described as being another thing, and consequently assuming some of its associations

myth story which explains the nature of things, without reference to historical circumstances

omniscient narrator a story-teller who assumes God-like knowledge

parable simple story which delivers a moral or lesson

pun two different meanings drawn from a single word

realism set of conventions which enables representation of knowable communities and knowable characters

rhetorical question a question asked for emphasis rather than enquiry

Romantic term applied to philosophical beliefs and artistic practices fashionable in Europe at the end of the eighteenth and beginning of the nineteenth century

simile overt comparison of one thing with another, in order to disclose shared attributes

social satire literature which mockingly exposes the flaws and foibles of society

type a representative figure

AUTHOR OF THIS NOTE

Dr Julian Cowley taught English at King's College London before joining the University of Luton, where he is Senior Lecturer in Literary Studies.

York Notes Advanced (£3.99 each)

Margaret Atwood
Cat's Eye

Margaret Atwood
The Handmaid's Tale

Jane Austen
Mansfield Park

Jane Austen
Persuasion

Jane Austen
Pride and Prejudice

Alan Bennett
Talking Heads

William Blake
Songs of Innocence and of Experience

Charlotte Brontë
Jane Eyre

Emily Brontë
Wuthering Heights

Angela Carter
Nights at the Circus

Geoffrey Chaucer
The Franklin's Prologue and Tale

Geoffrey Chaucer
The Miller's Prologue and Tale

Geoffrey Chaucer
Prologue To the Canterbury Tales

Geoffrey Chaucer
The Wife of Bath's Prologue and Tale

Samuel Taylor Coleridge
Selected Poems

Joseph Conrad
Heart of Darkness

Daniel Defoe
Moll Flanders

Charles Dickens
Great Expectations

Charles Dickens
Hard Times

Emily Dickinson
Selected Poems

John Donne
Selected Poems

Carol Ann Duffy
Selected Poems

George Eliot
Middlemarch

George Eliot
The Mill on the Floss

T.S. Eliot
Selected Poems

F. Scott Fitzgerald
The Great Gatsby

E.M. Forster
A Passage to India

Brian Friel
Translations

Thomas Hardy
The Mayor of Casterbridge

Thomas Hardy
The Return of the Native

Thomas Hardy
Selected Poems

Thomas Hardy
Tess of the d'Urbervilles

Seamus Heaney
Selected Poems from Opened Ground

Nathaniel Hawthorne
The Scarlet Letter

Kazuo Ishiguro
The Remains of the Day

Ben Jonson
The Alchemist

James Joyce
Dubliners

John Keats
Selected Poems

Christopher Marlowe
Doctor Faustus

Arthur Miller
Death of a Salesman

John Milton
Paradise Lost Books I & II

Toni Morrison
Beloved

Alexander Pope
Rape of the Lock and other poems

William Shakespeare
Antony and Cleopatra

William Shakespeare
As You Like It

William Shakespeare
Hamlet

William Shakespeare
King Lear

William Shakespeare
Measure for Measure

William Shakespeare
The Merchant of Venice

William Shakespeare
A Midsummer Night's Dream

William Shakespeare
Much Ado About Nothing

William Shakespeare
Othello

William Shakespeare
Richard II

William Shakespeare
Romeo and Juliet

William Shakespeare
The Taming of the Shrew

William Shakespeare
The Tempest

William Shakespeare
The Winter's Tale

George Bernard Shaw
Saint Joan

Mary Shelley
Frankenstein

Alice Walker
The Color Purple

Oscar Wilde
The Importance of Being Earnest

Tennessee Williams
A Streetcar Named Desire

John Webster
The Duchess of Malfi

Virginia Woolf
To the Lighthouse

W.B. Yeats
Selected Poems